Shadow of the Human

Shadow of the Human
An Adam Kind Alternate Future Mystery

K. R. Watts

Stuart Tartly Press

Stuart Tartly Press
17216 Saticoy Street, #226
Lake Balboa, CA 91406-2103

ISBN: 978-1-953595-12-6 (Hardcover edition)
ISBN: 978-1-953595-11-9 (Paperback edition)
ISBN: 978-1-953595-10-2 (eBook edition)

"The first principle is that you must not fool yourself,
and you are the easiest person to fool."
-Richard Feynman

"Bidden or not bidden, God is present."
-Carl Jung, quoting Erasmus, quoting a Delphic
Oracle.

Chapter 1

"Every member of society held multiple levels in various hierarchies: holder, tenant, or squatter; presbyter, pastor, or congregant; chosen or unchosen . . ."

Dorothy Kenning, *The Short Domination: A student primer*

It wasn't her.

I had thoroughly enjoyed the long ride in Brine's chariot, mercifully minus the company of Brine himself. We'd floated up from the San Fernando Valley, then inland, high over the Angeles forest, until we reached the high desert and the first view of our destination in the distance.

We had drifted downward then, until I could make out individual trees, the paths surrounding the complex, and finally a lone figure on the path below.

I caught my breath, and for a full second it seemed that the clouds had parted and sunlight glinted off the fresh snow—but only for a second.

Then I remembered the glint of monkstone light on bare metal.

The memory sent a shiver through me, and for another full second I forgot about the scene below.

I pushed the memory down where it came from, and a faint curiosity pulled me back to the view from my window. Curiosity, and a whisper of déjà vu.

She was walking away from me, down below, toward the Abbey. She wore a dark green cloak, with the hood up, so I couldn't even see the back of her head. It was all in the way she walked, the way she carried herself.

She put her suitcase down and paused to read a crooked wooden sign stuck in the ground by the side of the path, then picked the case up again and continued on her way.

I reached for my walking stick and rose from my seat, keeping my eyes on her back, as Brine's angel expertly navigated the chariot downward so that it came to hover an inch or less from the ground. If I had closed my eyes I wouldn't have guessed we were moving at all. The door swung silently open. I lifted my own suitcase and stepped out onto the gravel path, just as that green cloak rounded a corner and disappeared from my view.

The chariot lifted silently behind me and drifted off over the mountains.

I allowed myself a deep breath—and immediately regretted it as the icy air filled my lungs. I adjusted my scarf over my mouth and nose, took a few of the warmer breaths which that made possible, then began the trudge toward the Abbey.

Normally I would have delighted in the sound and feel of gravel underfoot, the snow-covered view, the scent of the woods —even the chance to celebrate Stonesday and Resurrection

Morning in an actual abbey. Normally, I could have enjoyed it thoroughly, even while hating my mission there.

But that day I was torn—pulled in multiple directions by duty, by worry, and by caution. And—still and silent beneath all of that—lay my personal reason for being there, which had nothing at all to do with my mission.

MY LIFE HAD BEEN SIMPLER, if not any lighter, until one night just the week before. Until then my darkness had all been personal and internal. The only practical difficulty I faced was a puzzle concerning my Aunt, which was straightforward enough even though it was proving difficult to solve.

Other than that my world moved predictably from Sunday services to weekday committee meetings, from afternoon counseling sessions to Thursday lunch at the Humble Monk, during which I would write the first draft of the next week's sermon. My week ran itself, and at times I could almost forget my own problems in the busyness of the days.

That Saturday evening Lucky and I were in the living room of our ancient Tudor parsonage on either side of the coffee table, having a game of Shadow. He had dealt me a very strong hand—a split run from L of clubs through P of hearts—and I was slowly working the bid up while trying not to scare him off.

Lucky was the only member of my staff. He had been almost a second father to me when I was growing up on the Franklyn estate, and he had had no place to go to when my father retired and the new manager brought his own people. So I took him in. I even gave him the larger of the two bedrooms in the parsonage. He took on the duties of cook and handyman. He wasn't chosen, but he knew his alphabet, and even without any formal education he was as good at Shadow as I was.

He ran a hand through his thinning hair, met my last raise, and raised again.

It looked like I was going to pull it off. I studied my cards, trying to give the impression that I wasn't sure what I wanted to do.

Lucky watched me in silence, his sharp features alert. Then he seemed to make a decision.

"There's a couple of things you ought to know, lad."

"About your hand?"

He shook his head.

"Not about the game."

I put my cards face down on the table.

"What?"

"The first is about you, and the second is about me. You'll be hearing from his holiness shortly."

"His holiness" was Lucky's nickname for Presbyter Brine, my immediate superior in the church. Lucky disliked him intensely, which was not an unusual reaction. Most people did.

"Is this one of your *hunches*?"

We didn't speak openly about Lucky's informant—his guardian angel, which had something of a divided agenda. It used Lucky to spy, first on my father and then on me. We didn't know for whom. But it also fed him information designed to keep him in my good graces.

If it had been human it would have guessed that Lucky was permanently in my good graces, but it wasn't human, and we gladly used whatever news it provided.

Lucky nodded.

"Brine's planning to send you on an errand, and it's not what it seems."

"Not what it seems?"

"He won't be telling you the whole story, lad. It's some kind of trap—or a test, at the very least."

"And that's as far as this hunch goes?"

"It's all I know. But you should be on your guard."

I picked up my cards, then I put them back down.

"You said 'a *couple* of things.' The other one was about you?"

He put his cards down now, as well.

"I'm going to be gone for a while."

I tensed. It was a statement, not a request.

"How long do you *want* to be gone for?"

"It will take as long as it takes."

"And where do you want to go?"

"To the city, to start with. After that, wherever I need to."

"Why?"

"That's private."

I forced myself to breathe. This was something I had never anticipated.

"Be reasonable, Lucky. If you expect me to give you permission to be gone for some undetermined time without even knowing where you'll be, you have to at least tell me why—"

"I don't."

"You *do* need to. I can't give—"

"I mean I don't expect you to give me permission, lad. I have to do this, permission or not."

I held myself under control.

"Let me sleep on this," I said, "and we can talk again tomorrow."

I picked up my cards, but my hands were shaking. Insubordination from Lucky wasn't something I was prepared to deal with.

I met his raise without speaking.

He turned his hand over.

A solid run. *U* through *Y* of diamonds.

He flashed me an apologetic smile as he pulled in his tokens.

I HAD CLIMBED the stairs without saying goodnight.

I was too angry to sleep, so I locked myself in my study and slumped in my desk chair.

Normally I would have taken the matter to prayer, but that was impossible at the moment, so I contemplated the sculpture on the wall opposite my desk instead.

It was a gift from Presbyter Brine. A token, he had said—between all his characteristic digressions and "ahhhs"—a token of my promising future in the church.

The artist was talented, and it was indeed a thing of beauty. It was titled "The Great Chain." At the top was an image of Joshua on his throne, carved from stone and inlaid with iron and gold. Three links hung from the bottom of the throne—one each of iron, of stone, and of gold.

The central link of the three, carved from stone, supported a chain, or network, of more and smaller stone links, representing the structure of the church. It separated into the various denominations and orders, and even exhibited something of their internal structures.

The right-hand link was the first in a similar chain of iron—representing the government, the iron rod of the police and enforcement of the law.

The left-hand link, of gold, supported a chain representing the structure of the *holders'* world, all the various corporations and wealthy families and their intricate ties.

As a whole, it exhibited the divinely ordained order of creation. The lines of responsibility and obedience that structured the world and gave it form.

Lucky had violated that pattern. My responsibility was to provide for him and to protect him; his, to obey me.

That was what *justified* my fury, but I wasn't sure what drove it. I had the distinct impression that my anger was rooted elsewhere.

Was I was terrified of losing Lucky, after losing Bee? Possibly.

Was I jealous that Lucky could defy me openly in the way that I would like to defy Presbyter Brine, but couldn't? Perhaps.

Was I angry that Lucky had handed me a situation I didn't have the slightest idea how to cope with? Certainly.

Or was it that I knew I *had*, in fact, defied Brine, and the law, and I knew I shouldn't have?

I glanced at the wainscoting next to my chair. You couldn't see where the hole had been before the repairs. The hole that I had never reported to the police, the hole which would have exposed a killer.

I looked back at the Bible sitting on my desk—the Bible that also contained my family journals, which I had promised to turn over to Brine. A promise I had never intended to keep.

I focused once more on the sculpture, the Great Chain of Being.

I had violated that pattern as well, more subtly than Lucky had, and perhaps my sin was worse because of that.

Perhaps.

But none of that told me what to do about Lucky.

Chapter 2

"The fact that the 'Humans' managed, for hundreds of years, to survive and even to thrive within the relentless repression of the short domination borders on the inconceivable."

Dorothy Kenning, *The Short Domination: A student primer*

I FOLLOWED the woman in the green cloak toward the abbey, passing the sign she had stopped to peruse:

SAINT ISSAC'S ABBEY
NO HUNTING
EXCEPT FOR TRUTH

I read it absently, still thinking about Lucky.

Bee would have helped me. She would have known how to handle Lucky.

She would probably have irritated the hell out of me in the process, but she would also probably have been right. Every time we argued about theology, *she* convinced *me*—the seminary graduate—not the other way around. Even when I wouldn't admit it.

It was so odd to think that only a few months ago Bee had been no more to me than a faint memory of a childhood playmate. That first day she'd walked into the Humble Monk as an adult woman, I hadn't even recognized her.

I turned the same corner the woman in green had turned, and saw her approaching the entrance to the Abbey ahead of me.

She stepped up onto the porch of the main building—a long, low structure with a chimney that actually emitted smoke.

I could smell it then on the air, and it made me reassess my mission. Why would Brine have sent me—a mere local pastor at the very beginning of my career in the church—sent *me* on a sensitive mission to a prestigious abbey. An abbey important enough to be allowed a real, wood-burning, fireplace?

Off to my left I could see what appeared to be a small chapel. Not far from that was a large gong, possibly eight feet in diameter, probably used for calling the monks to services.

A monk stood beside it, a very tall man with slightly hunched shoulders. He was peering intently at the woman in green.

Apparently I was not the only one curious about her.

But I was more than curious. There was something in the way she stood, the way she moved, even disguised by that green cloak.

Something familiar.

I watched as she disappeared through the front door. When I turned my attention back to the monk, he had vanished.

I HADN'T TALKED to Lucky the morning after our card game. I used the Sunday services and my duties at church as an excuse to avoid him. And I avoided him Monday morning, as well. I left the parsonage as soon as I got up and went straight to the Humble Monk for breakfast.

The Humble Monk was something of a sanctuary for me. I experienced a kind of solitude there, eating and reading my Bible, insulated from the rest of the world by the clatter of plates, the odor of pastries and coffee, the counterpoint of conversations straining to be heard above the blare of gospel music from the proprietor's Bible.

I indulged in a latte, and considered Saturday night's conversation over a plate of bacon and pancakes.

I still didn't have a clue what to do about Lucky's plan or his insubordination—so I turned my attention to his other announcement. Apparently I should be expecting to hear from Brine.

Lucky had said Brine would have an "errand" for me. I had no idea what that would entail, but knowing Brine it was likely to be intrusive and time-consuming, if not professionally dangerous. So I made a list in my Bible of pressing business I needed to wind up before he contacted me.

Aunt Joan was at the top of my list. I had no idea how I was going to make any progress on that puzzle, but it was an important obligation. The longer it was left unresolved, the heavier it weighed on me.

So after breakfast I stopped by the police station. The

officer on the front desk waved me through the door to the back of the building.

The hallway leading to Dennis's office was a pleasant beige, and still smelled of fresh paint. I made my way about halfway down the hall and stopped in front of his office. The sign on the door read *Dennis Troy, Chief of Police.*

I knocked, and Dennis's voice answered from within.

"Come."

His new office was much larger than the dingy little room he had occupied until recently as a mere detective. Unlike the hallway, it hadn't needed a new coat of paint. The walls still sported the expensive paintings the previous occupant had hung there, and Dennis's round dark visage beamed at me from behind the former chief's enormous desk.

He leaned back in his predecessor's tooled leather chair and motioned me to sit. His silver hair, against the background of the leather, lent the chair a dignity that its former occupant had never achieved.

"Coffee?"

"No thanks, I just had breakfast."

"You sure? It's worth drinking now. One of my departmental reforms . . ."

The furrow between his eyes deepened, and he grinned.

". . . and maybe the most important one."

I laughed.

"Oh I don't know. Those beige hallways are pretty impressive. I see you kept the art."

He gave the walls a thoughtful scan.

"I haven't decided yet. They're not really my taste, but they give the office a certain gravitas. Only they remind me every day of Tho. Like he's haunting the place. But I don't think the department budget would stretch to replacements."

"You could always sell those, or trade them for something you liked."

"Now there's a thought."

He gave an absent nod, then met my eyes.

"Is this a social call?"

"I wish it were. I'm afraid I need to bug you about any progress on my aunt."

"I doubt it, but let me look."

He leaned forward and pulled his Bible toward him. He signed it open, then moved his stylus across its surface.

After some time he looked up.

"Nothing, I'm afraid. To be fair, we haven't given them much to go on. A first name that may or may not be real. A second name that almost certainly isn't. The fact that she visited servants at the Franklyn estate during several summers a decade ago, and was a close friend of the estate manager's wife, who is no longer with us. It's not much of a starting point."

"I get it," I said. "And the probability that she's a 'Human' . . ."

"Makes it worse, not better—in two ways. First, it makes it less likely that we'll find anything, since we have no idea where Humans live, or really any information about them at all."

"We know that they refuse to wear a logo."

"And that they wear fake logos when they can be seen in public. Or pretend to be holders without logos. In other words, they could look like just about anyone."

"Still . . ."

"And second, it loses us cooperation. You and I are convinced they exist, because of what we witnessed a couple of months ago, but for most people—including most of our professionals—asking them to track a capital 'H' Human is like asking them to track a leprechaun. They don't put their whole energy into it, if you see what I mean."

He shook his head and furrowed his brow again.

"The truth is, I've stopped including any reference to the 'Human' thing. It's counterproductive."

"I see. Well, I've got to find her, somehow."

"Oh, I'll keep trying, but I wouldn't put anything else on hold for it if I were you."

He paused, assessing my mood, then asked, "How are you doing otherwise?"

He was referring to my grief. He didn't know anything about my other problem.

"As well as can be expected, I guess. It'll take time. That's what everyone tells me."

He nodded.

"We should have lunch soon."

***

The woman in green was nowhere to be seen when I entered the Abbey. The front door opened onto a large common room. A fire blazed in the fireplace at the far end. Couches and deep comfortable chairs were arranged by the fire, and a couple of large tables dominated the center of the room. The back wall had floor-to-ceiling windows, looking out onto the snow-covered hillside behind the building. The floor was carpeted, and the walls were lined with artwork, mostly on religious themes.

A bare Solstice Tree stood in one corner, waiting to be decorated on Resurrection Morning.

A light-skinned, blue-eyed fellow in a monk's habit, somewhat younger than myself, approached as I entered. He asked if I were Pastor Kinde. I said I was.

He smiled.

"I'm Brother Earnest. If you'll follow me, I'll take you to your room."

He led the way out a back door into the cold again and along a path between the building and the hillside. Eventually we came to some stone steps which led up the hill to a series of small buildings, each housing two guest rooms.

The rooms had names painted on their doors: Faith, Hope, Truth, etc.

He brought me to the door of my room, which was labeled "Obedience".

I wondered if God appreciated irony.

The room itself was simple. It was about twelve feet square. It had a tile floor and contained a narrow bed, a small dresser, and a single wooden chair. A ceramic plaque above the dresser depicted the stone heap. A row of high windows along the top of one wall provided natural light. All I could see through them was sky.

A door on one wall led to a small room containing a toilet, a sink, and a shower.

Brother Earnest smiled again.

"I wouldn't leave any showers to the morning. We tend to run out of hot water then."

"Thanks for the warning."

"You're welcome to attend services with the community while you're here, and to make use of the common room where you came in. Meals are served in the refectory, which you can enter through the doors from the common room. The gong rings for services, the bell for meals. The Abbot's office has its own entrance from the front porch of that same building. The Abbot will be expecting you after lunch."

He paused to catch his breath and seemed to be going over the speech in his head, to make sure he hadn't left anything out.

"Oh! And you're free to wander down the path to the

entrance, around the pond, or up the hiking path to the cemetery. But the rest of the grounds are private to the monks unless
you have the Abbot's permission—including, of course, the path
to the hermitage, which you'll pass if you go to the cemetery."

He flashed me one last smile.

"Any questions?"

"Not at the moment, Brother Earnest."

"I'll leave you to get settled then."

He closed the door behind him as he left.

Chapter 3

"The average holder was no more privy to the purposes or strategies of power than any other. Like their tenants, the clergy, the police, or even the squatters on their land, they held to the rules of the society on moral grounds. For the most part they oppressed others because they believed it was the moral thing to do."

Dorothy Kenning, *The Short Domination: A student primer*

I SPENT A FEW MINUTES UNPACKING, then grabbed my stick and Bible to go exploring.

Presbyter Brine had suggested that I keep to the main Abbey grounds—ignoring the cemetery, hermitage, and other parts of the property in my investigation. So after a brief visit to the pond—which was iced over—I headed up the hiking path to the cemetery.

Which was, quite possibly, exactly what Brine had intended.

The path felt a bit barren to me at first. I eventually realized it was because I lived in a populated area, where there was always a building of some sort in view, and always a statue of Joshua as well. Once that was clear to me I found the emptiness calming.

After a while the path began to rise more steeply, and I was glad I had brought my walking stick. I didn't actually carry it because I needed it, or because it was fashionable, even though it was. I carried it because it was my father's and because Bee had liked it. But it was useful on that hill.

At the top of the rise the path split and went in two directions. There was a sign, lettered like the one I had seen coming in, pointing to the left and the cemetery. Another one, by the other branch of the path, simply read:

PLEASE RESPECT

THE SOLITUDE

OF THE HERMIT.

Between the paths stood a statue of Joshua. It was a different style than the ones in my village, probably produced by the Abbey itself.

The path to the hermitage was straight, so I could see the tiny stone cottage it led to. It had a small porch at the front, on which sat a single chair. A single window and a single door opened onto the porch.

As I watched, a man emerged from the door. He wore a simple monk's robe. It was difficult to judge his age, because the robe hid the shape of his body and because his hair and beard were both long. Extremely long.

He was carrying a tea-cup. He brushed the snow off of the porch railing, and poured something from the cup onto the bare wood. Then he stepped back until he was leaning against the closed door, and watched. After a short time several birds appeared to feast on whatever he had put there.

He saw me as he turned to go back inside and paused to stare my way. I didn't know whether it was proper protocol to wave, so I waited. He didn't wave either, but he also didn't move, so after a time I decided it was up to me.

I lifted my hand in greeting, and was immediately interrupted.

"FEAR NOT!"

There was an angel standing by my side.

When I was a boy in seminary, and saw the head's guardian angel on a regular basis, that phrase would have made me laugh. But on this lonely path, in someone else's territory, and not expecting anything of the kind, it nearly startled me out of my skin.

The angel didn't wait for me to recover.

"Please respect the solitude of the hermit."

It was apparently going to stick to the script.

"You may use this path to visit the cemetery, but please respect—"

"—the solitude of the hermit," I said.

"Fine," I said, "I will."

The angel vanished, and a quick glance toward the hermitage told me that the hermit was gone as well.

I thought about visiting the cemetery, then, but the bell rang for lunch.

THE COMMON ROOM was filled with a rumble of conversations. A crowd had gathered in anticipation of the midday meal. I worked my way to the back corner, by the Solstice Tree.

It gave off a strong scent of pine, which I hadn't noticed when I arrived, probably because of the wood fire at the other end of the room. This mingled with the aromas of food coming from behind the closed doors of the dining room.

There was a window in the corner. A thin, frail monk sat motionless in a chair placed in front of it, staring at the snow-covered vista outside. He could have passed for a hundred and eighty, easily.

Brother Earnest joined me, and asked if I'd had a chance to explore.

"I wandered up the hiking path a way, as far as the path to the hermitage."

He smiled.

"Did you get a glimpse of our hermit?"

"I did, actually, and got reprimanded by his guardian angel when I waved to him."

"His angel can be quite intimidating. But its bark is worse than its bite. We're all quite proud of our hermit. Not every abbey has one."

"How long has he been here?"

"Only a couple of years. He arrived about the same time I did."

"I would have guessed much longer, from the length of his beard."

He chuckled at that.

The doors to the dining room opened, and the crowd began to move.

"Do you happen to know," I asked, "who the woman was who arrived just before I did?"

"Sister Edith? She's here on retreat. You didn't recognize her?"

"Is she famous?"

A nervous little laugh escaped him.

"No. It's just . . . I thought you knew her."

"Oh? Why?"

"Because she asked if you had arrived yet. When she came in."

"Really? I did think there was something familiar about her. Maybe I'll see her at lunch and clear up the mystery."

"You won't. She's eating in solitude. Part of her retreat. Joshuans have some odd customs."

His hand went to his mouth and he blushed.

"Forgive me. I shouldn't be talking like that in front of a guest of the abbey."

"It's all right. I won't report you. So she's a Joshuan?"

The Joshuan Order held a very special place in that chain of being which hung on the wall of my study.

They were prestigious without being powerful—at least not in any ordinary sense. They had a seat on the supreme religious council, and their representative always attended, but never took part in the debates, and never exercised their vote.

They had a reputation as deeply mystical, though the peculiarities of their mysticism were unknown to outsiders.

And, unlike all other orders and denominations, they took no money from the council, in spite of the fact that they had a large number of houses spread across the country. They supported themselves through their own labor, and through direct donations from holders friendly to the order.

And they kept almost entirely to themselves. Even a member of the clergy could go his entire life without ever meeting one.

Which, until that day, I believed I had done.

The dining room had only a single long table which seated everyone in the community. Brother Earnest and I sat at the end nearest the door, since we were the last to arrive.

The Abbot stood at the other end of the table and rang a small bell, at which point everyone ceased talking and the room was engulfed in silence.

I was surprised to see that the Abbot was a woman.

She was very short, very round, and exuded an air of complete authority.

She uttered a brief prayer of thanks then took her own seat, next to the tall monk I had seen on my way in.

We were served a steaming bowl of onion soup, a hunk of freshly baked bread, and a small salad.

It was tasty, warming, and nourishing.

Lucky couldn't have done better.

AFTER MY CONVERSATION about Aunt Joan with Dennis at the police station on Monday, I had been in no mood for church work, so I had decided to try to get help on my other problem—Lucky's sudden defiant attitude.

I hopped on my chariot and floated it along the dusty road next to squatter territory until I came to the Franklyn estate—a green oasis in the brown world outside of the village.

I wanted to talk with Boyd Franklyn, who had a lot more experience dealing with servants than I did.

Boyd was welcoming as always. We had grown up together on the estate, where my father had served his father, and most of the time he treated me as an equal. He ushered me into his library, and I explained the situation.

"You just can't allow it. That's all."

Boyd was grinning, but it wasn't a grin of amusement. The very idea of insubordination in a servant made him furious.

"I understand that much," I said, "but how, exactly, do I *go about* not allowing it?"

"You forbid him to go. You restrict him to the parsonage."

"And if he leaves anyway?"

"He wouldn't dare."

"I think he would."

"After all you've done for him?"

Boyd had a point. Only two months ago Lucky had been in prison and on trial for murder. It had been left to me to defend him, and though I was not particularly proud of my performance, he had been acquitted. And, of course, I had also kept secrets for Lucky that even Boyd knew nothing about.

I shrugged.

"I just think he feels he has to do this at whatever cost. Maybe I should just give him permission. Then he wouldn't be disobeying me."

Boyd shook his head.

"Maybe, if he hadn't already crossed the line, but you can't do that now."

"It wouldn't have to set a precedent."

"It would though. I know how you feel about Lucky, Adam. Hell, I feel the same way. He was an unofficial uncle to both of us growing up. But this is bigger than Lucky. You have a responsibility to society to hold the line. You may not see that with only one servant, and one you're so close to, but it's true."

"So *how?*"

He stroked his beard in thought.

"You'll have to tell him that if he goes he can't come back. At this point that's the only leverage you've got."

"I don't know if I can do that."

"You do realize that you can't allow a servant to return after going off without your permission?"

"I suppose . . ."

"So don't you think you owe it to him to give him advance warning?"

Chapter 4

> "It's generally agreed that Kinde's second adventure was also a turning point for him personally. There is, however, very little agreement as to the nature of that turning point."

Silas Redford, *The Real Adam Kinde: An Experiment in Biography*

I KNOCKED at the Abbot's door after breakfast, and she called for me to enter.

Her office was a bit larger than mine back at the parsonage. The doorway and one large window took up all of the front wall, giving her a grand view of the front garden of the Abbey, including the path I had arrived by and glimpses between the trees of the snow-covered hills beyond.

The walls on both sides were lined with shelves, containing all sorts of strange objects—most of which I couldn't identify. I did recognize a triangular light crystal and a firmament viewer, because of my brief exposure to such things in seminary, but all the rest were a mystery to me.

The back wall sported a single, large painting of the Abbey. Next to it hung a gold-plated throwing knife, mounted on a wooden plaque.

The room had an odd smell that reminded me of the cleaning solutions Lucky sometimes used.

In the center of the room there was a round table, surrounded by four very comfortable chairs.

The Abbot sat in the chair at the back of the table, facing the window and the door. Her hair was black with streaks of grey. Her complexion was reddish and freckled. She seemed taller, sitting, than she had seemed standing at the end of the table at lunch, but not much. Her logo, tattooed over her left eyebrow like my own, depicted a maiden wielding a sword.

So she was an Arcite.

That explained how a woman came to be Abbot. The Arcites were a celibate order of women whose callings were to roles usually filled by men.

Her order was further confirmed by the fact that she was dressed as a monk rather than as a sister, and by the stone which hung from a beautifully worked chain around her neck— an unpolished stone whose rough edges were tinged with red to represent the blood of Joshua.

My own stone, which also hung from a neck chain, was polished smooth and worn inside my clothes, against my skin, as was the custom with Fundamentalists, who accused Arcites of reveling in the suffering of Joshua—while they accused us of worshiping the instrument of his torture rather than his sacrifice.

Her Bible lay on the table in front of her, along with three other objects which were as strange to me as any of those on the shelves.

She motioned for me to sit in the chair facing her.

Faintly, through the closed door, I could hear the wind-chimes I had passed on the porch outside.

"Welcome to Saint Isaac's Abbey, Pastor. How can we serve you?"

I steeled myself for the role I had to play.

"I'm here on a fact-finding mission for the local Fundamentalist presbytery. We're studying various other denominations and orders to see if they have practices or structures worth adopting."

I wasn't happy about lying, even under orders, but there it was.

She smiled—a bit indulgently—and I suddenly found myself wondering if a lie was really a sin if you knew you weren't believed.

"You are aware that we are a research abbey, and that any information about most of what we do—and about how we do it—requires a rather high level of access?"

I nodded, and extended my right hand toward her, palm out.

She held her Bible against my palm for a moment, turned it back to face her, scribbled something with her stylus, and failed to hide her look of surprise.

"May I ask your rank?"

"I'm a village pastor."

"Really?"

I nodded.

"And that," she said, "is all?"

I nodded again.

"It's my first position."

"And you've been sent here?"

"Yes."

"With access just one level below my own?"

"If that's what it says."

"On a 'fact-finding mission' for your presbytery?"

"Exactly."

"And you expect me to believe that?"

"I'm just following orders."

That seemed to amuse her.

"I see. Orders about what to do, or orders about how much to tell me, I wonder. And I'm to believe you have no other reason for being here?"

I decided to take the opening and use it to change the subject.

"Actually, there is another reason."

"And that is?"

"I'm also in need of spiritual counseling."

Her manner changed abruptly, from skepticism to concern.

"What kind of spiritual counseling?"

"I seem to have been abandoned."

"Abandoned?"

"By God."

FROM THE TIME I first began to pray, prayer had been a two-way conversation for me. I don't mean that I "heard voices" or anything like that. I just never felt alone or as though I was praying into a void.

I would pour out my concerns, ask for guidance, sometimes even ask for intervention, and I always sensed a listening ear at the other end.

The interventions, if they came at all, were always questionable to me.

One particularly dry season a friend confided in me that he had been praying for rain for six months when "God finally answered his prayer".

He thought the rain, when it came, was a tribute to his faithfulness, his ability to soldier on in prayer in spite of how long it took to get results.

I was young and a bit naïve at the time, so—instead of biting my tongue—I pointed out that it probably was always going to rain sooner or later.

He wouldn't speak to me for a month.

But even at that young age I could see that most "answered prayers" of that type were a matter of interpretation.

What was not, for me, a matter of interpretation was my direct experience of God.

When I prayed I *experienced* God listening to me. That's as clear as I can put it. It was a palpable presence for me. I could count on God's ear, and it changed the way I prayed. I found it impossible to lie to God, and by extension to myself, about anything I brought to prayer.

Quite probably that explained my inability to rationalize "answers to prayer" like my friends did.

I would bring a problem to God, and as I poured out my concerns I would find myself noticing all my rationalizations, all the things I *wanted* to believe but had no good evidence for. I could sense the silent questions in the quality of God's listening, and I would find myself backtracking, modifying my views, seeing how I was contributing to the problem I had brought, or how others might view it.

And I would always come away changed.

I would come away centered, with greater compassion for others and with greater insight into myself.

Then one day I tried to pray, and God wasn't there.

I no longer had any sense that God was listening. Prayer had become simply talking to myself—or to a void. What had once been a presence had become an absence.

It was like being deep in conversation with a friend, only to look up and see that they had left the room some time ago.

The touchstone that had guided me from boyhood was gone.

The Abbot listened patiently while I attempted to explain all of this, occasionally making a note in her Bible, and only very occasionally asking a clarifying question.

When I had finished, she regarded me thoughtfully.

"Well, that is quite a story. I have several things to say to you in response."

She paused to collect her thoughts, then continued, ticking each point off on her fingers.

"I think the first thing is to tell you that I believe you. I don't believe the rubbish about your mission here, and I think you knew that already. But I do believe that you are experiencing an absence of God, and I do believe that your request for help is sincere.

"The second thing I have to tell you is that your experience is not unusual. In fact, it's quite common. So, as painful as this is for you, you are not alone.

"Third, I'll try to get you the help you need. Unfortunately, we don't have a resident counselor at the moment. But I have someone in mind who at one point went through a similar experience, and who I think may be able to help, if he will agree to try.

"And the final thing I have to say is that while I don't believe a word of your story about your mission, I *do* believe that you are 'just following orders' and have no choice in the matter. I also find myself trusting you. So I'm going to take a chance and give you the access you want. And I'm going to trust that you will use that access fairly and wisely."

So that is how I successfully navigated the first part of my mission—and how I came to hope fervently that the Abbot herself had nothing at all to do with it.

I HAD FINALLY LEARNED what that mission was only three days earlier.

"This will . . . ahhh, do . . . will do nicely, I think."

"This" had been a bench in the village park. Presbyter Brine had been gasping for breath from the exertion of walking, and his face was even redder than usual. Why, in his condition, he had insisted that we conduct our conversation outdoors and on foot was a mystery.

He sagged his enormous bulk onto the bench, breathing raggedly, and gestured for me to sit beside him.

The bench was damp, but I sat anyway.

I waited for him to catch his breath. It was chilly out, but the sky was bright blue without a cloud, and the park, empty except for the two of us, was lovely. It had rained the night before, and everything was unusually green.

It had been almost a week since Lucky had warned me to expect this visit, and I was anxious to know the worst.

Brine's panting slowed somewhat, and he finally spoke.

"I think that you, as you probably . . . ahhh . . . probably know . . . I think you have a promising career before you."

"I'm flattered, sir."

"Not at all . . . It's quite . . . ahhh . . . tell me . . . how would *you* define 'heresy'?"

I was immediately on my guard.

"Heresy?"

"Yes. How would you . . . what would you say distinguish-es . . . in your view . . . what is it that makes a belief heretical?"

I chose my words carefully.

"As I understand it, sir, heresy is simply the holding of a false doctrine."

"Ahhh. Yes. But what, exactly is it . . . what *qualifies* a doctrine as false?"

This was very dangerous ground, and I feared I was about to step into a trap.

"I'm afraid I don't understand, sir."

He fixed an eye on me, and was silent for several panting breaths before he continued.

"When I was a young man . . . perhaps a little older than you, but still young . . . there was a raging debate over whether . . . ahhh . . . whether Joshua *knew* that he was divine . . . knew while he was growing up, you see . . . knew that he was the son of God.

"There were those who argued that he *didn't* . . . ahhh . . . couldn't have known . . . that it would have been incompatible with his . . . his humanity, you see. Have you heard of this before?"

"Never."

"Excellent. More helpful if you haven't. I, as it turned out, was on the right side of the . . . ahhh . . . the debate. I argued that he . . . and this is important . . . he *must* have known . . . must have known *because* the scriptures record that he called God 'father.'"

"Very insightful. It goes right to the heart of the matter."

"That's the . . . ahhh . . . the point, you see. It didn't . . . *didn't* go to the heart of the matter. Missed it completely. Saved me a great deal of . . . ahhh . . . of embarrassment, of course. No need to recant a heretical position. But I had chosen the correct position for the . . . for the wrong reason."

I wished he would get on with it. I could already feel the damp from the bench penetrating my slacks.

"What," I asked, "would have been the *right* reason?"

"That is the question I would like you to contemplate, in preparation for the . . . the . . . ahhh . . . the task before you."

Chapter 5

> "Heresy, a capital offense for all but the clergy, was in practice a charge used for political rather than doctrinal reasons."

Dorothy Kenning, *The Short Domination: A student primer*

"I THINK that concludes our official business," the Abbot said. "I'll give you a tour of the Abbey tomorrow, after breakfast. Would you like to stay for a cup of tea?"

"Thank you. I would."

She busied herself at a small altar in the corner of the office while I puzzled over the strange objects on her desk. When she returned with our tea, I nodded toward them.

"I take it your vocation is not merely administration?"

"I'm a member of the Yerubian Guild, if that means anything to you."

"You're a fleecer, then. Deep theology. I sometimes wish I had taken that path."

"It's fascinating work." She gestured at all the objects on the shelves. "I like to keep a hand in, even though most of my energy is taken up with the Abbey's business these days."

"I'd like to hear more about it while I'm here, if you have the time."

She shot me an appraising look.

"Well, you certainly have the access."

"I hadn't thought of it that way. I suppose this may be a once-in-a-lifetime opportunity."

She abruptly changed the subject.

"I have another appointment in a few minutes—with someone I think you know."

"Really?"

"She apparently asked about you when she arrived."

"Oh. The mysterious Sister Edith."

"Mysterious?"

"I have no idea who she is, or where I could know her from. I saw her walking up the path ahead of me when I arrived, and she did look vaguely familiar to me—from the back. But Brother Earnest tells me that she's a Joshuan, and I don't think I've ever met a Joshuan."

"Few people have. Why don't you stay when she comes, and perhaps you can solve the mystery—in fact, here she is now."

She called out toward the door.

"Come on in, dear. No need to knock!"

I turned in my seat and saw a woman enter who was close to my own age and height.

Her hair was black, long, and braided. It was encircled by a white headband, which had the Joshuan logo embroidered just above her left eye. Her habit was the same dark green as the cloak she had worn that morning. It was an unusually loose style, and made her look smaller than she was, as though she were dressed in her mother's clothes.

It gave her an air of vulnerability.

She wore her stone on a bracelet rather than a necklace. It was rough-cut and unpolished, but it had been shaped into something like a tear-drop. There was no red on it. The bracelet was made of large metal links in a design that felt vaguely familiar to me. But I didn't focus on that because her eyes met mine, and she smiled in recognition.

"Hello Adam."

I returned the smile.

"Hello Lilith."

"It's 'Sister Edith' now."

I grinned.

"Hello Sister Edith, then."

"So," said the Abbot, "you *do* know each other."

"Lilith—Sister Edith—and I were close friends during my senior year at seminary."

Lilith chuckled.

"*Very* close friends."

I sighed—and probably blushed.

"Yes. We were very close."

Lilith met the Abbot's eyes.

"Adam lived off-campus that year, you see."

The Abbot was amused.

"I *do* see."

Lilith was enjoying herself.

"So," I said, "you're a Joshuan now?"

"And you're a pastor."

"I am."

The Abbot gestured toward the teapot.

"Would you like to join us? Or would you rather see me in private?"

"Oh, it's nothing confidential. Some tea would be lovely."

The Abbot poured.

"What can I do for you?"

"It's not about my retreat. A personal favor, actually."

"I'm intrigued."

"You are—or were—Margaret Cavendish?"

"I am still. We don't change our names when we join the order."

"Winner of the Brumbach Prize?"

The Abbot nodded toward the plaque on the wall.

Lilith continued.

"I was hoping you could give me a demonstration, and maybe even a lesson, while I'm here?"

"I don't think so. I only throw as a recreation now, and only in private." She smiled and shrugged. "Sorry."

I WAS sure that wouldn't be the end of it.

Lilith generally got her way. She could always talk anyone into anything.

Anyone. Not just me.

Bee had been able to talk me into anything at all, but that was because I was in love with her—even before I knew I was.

With Lilith it was a talent. A talent she could use on anyone at a moment's notice.

I wondered if I had ever really been in love with Lilith. It was possible she'd just convinced me I was. It certainly hadn't been like it was with Bee.

They were alike in many ways, though. Not fundamentally, but in little ways.

Their smiles were similar.

I'd missed Bee's smile.

I remembered the first time I saw it—the first time I saw Bee as an adult—when we exchanged that uncomfortable glance in the Humble Monk—uncomfortable for me, anyway.

I hadn't recognized *her* then, either.

Just like I hadn't recognized Lilith on the walk into the Abbey.

I should have known that walk anywhere, but I didn't.

Maybe that was my type, if I had one: women I didn't recognize.

EVERY TIME I met Presbyter Brine I came away confused.

That morning we sat together on the park bench had been no exception. As I listened to his instructions, I kept wondering whether he was coiled to strike or whether he was just offering me a nice, tasty apple.

I did know that the damp green scent of the park and the clear blue sky did not make up for the discomfort of the wet bench.

Or for my discomfort at the task he was assigning me.

". . . It's just that I don't feel I'm quite ready, sir. For this level of assignment. I wouldn't want to be responsible for the outcome. I've only been a pastor for a very short time, and—"

"—Allow me" Brine interrupted, "to correct you on that point, Pastor. What you are not quite . . . or, in fact, *at all* ready for is to question the judgment of your superiors. It is not your . . . ahhh . . . your *place* to worry about the outcome. Your job is obedience. The outcome will take . . . take care of itself."

He fixed me with a dominant glare before continuing.

"Your . . . ahhh . . . your *official* reason will be a fact-finding mission. A mission for the presbytery. Learning about how the Abbey operates . . . finding what we can adopt."

"And my real mission?"

"I see you follow me. Excellent. We . . . my superiors and I . . . we have reason . . . ahhh . . . *good* reason to believe that there are heretics there."

"Is that unusual? I would think you could find quite a few right here in the village."

"In *this* village?"

"Yes, sir. Some who know they are and don't care, but a great many more who have no idea that their views are heretical at all. I wouldn't be surprised to learn that even I hold some views that aren't quite sound, doctrinally."

"Ahhh. Or even myself?"

"I didn't mean to imply—"

"No. You are quite right, of course. I'm impressed at your . . . at your . . . ahhh . . . your insight. Heresy is unavoidable, of course. But there are . . . ahhh . . . heresies, and then there are *heresies*, if you take my meaning."

"Some are more dangerous than others."

"Exactly, and some . . . some *heretics* are more dangerous than others."

"And that is the kind of heretic you think—"

"—is being harbored by the Abbey."

"And my task?"

"Your task is to use your position there . . . your position as a fact-finder for the presbytery, to befriend, observe, deduce, and . . . ahhh . . . expose the heretics."

"Expose them to . . . "

"To myself. In your report, when you return."

"What, exactly, is the heresy I'm looking for?"

"We have . . . ahhh . . . have *some* idea, of course, but nothing . . . nothing *definitive.* I wouldn't want to prejudice your search. But I will give you two names . . . two names we particularly suspect, and warn you about . . . about one person you would be wise to avoid completely."

I'd nodded. The back of my slacks were already soaked through.

Chapter 6

"The end of the Second Enlightenment was marked by a political, economic, and religious consolidation, but even more by the absorption of science by theology."

Lois Bradford, *An Introduction to the Second Enlightenment*

BRINE WOULD HAVE CONSIDERED my first day at the Abbey to be a mixed performance.

I had met and, I thought, had successfully befriended one of his two main suspects just as I had been instructed to do. I had also had my access accepted, which would give me the latitude I would need for the rest of my task.

All of that would have pleased him, I was sure.

On the other hand, I had gone out of my way to get a glimpse of the one person he had advised me to avoid.

I didn't know how he would feel about that. Brine was

capable of deep and complex manipulation. He may have warned me about the hermit precisely in order to arouse my curiosity.

But my job wasn't to speculate. It was to follow orders.

I had no idea what he would have made of my meeting an old girl-friend. Probably nothing at all. She wasn't a resident at the Abbey, so it was extremely unlikely that she had anything to do with my mission. But that didn't keep me from wondering about her.

The Abbot had arranged to give me a tour of the Abbey after breakfast the following morning, so we met in the common room, and she led me out the front door, along the porch, and down a stone path which had been shoveled clear of snow.

As we made our way down the path, I thanked her for taking the time to show me around personally.

She shrugged.

"It's really no bother. I take a walk after breakfast most mornings, so this will just take its place."

"Where do you usually walk?"

"To the graveyard, or up the path you arrived by, and along the road it leads to. There's an estate not far up that road, so it's kept in fairly good condition."

The path took us past the chapel to a large two-story building made of brick.

It was round, windowless, and had only a single entrance that I could see.

The Abbot traced a quick circle in the air in front of the entrance panel at the side of the door, then tugged on the handle to let us in.

We entered a long broad hallway, lit by sky-lights from above and by the light of an inner courtyard from the other end. The walls were a mosaic of theological themes. Very little from the life of Joshua, or the history of his church. Much more from what I took to be deep theology, ranging from scenes I could recognize from the scriptures to symbols and images I didn't recognize at all.

It was all quite well done, though. The artist, or artists, had created an impression which was at once beautiful and awe-inspiring.

I would have liked to stop and admire it, but the Abbot kept walking, so I hurried on and caught up with her just as we emerged into a courtyard.

The courtyard gave me a sense of just how large the circle of the building must be. It was, itself, circular, and must have been close to a hundred yards in diameter. It contained trees, paved areas with benches and sculptures, an iced-over reflecting pool, and snow-covered areas that were probably gardens during the summer.

It was surrounded by a wide covered walkway, which led around the inside of the building proper—past the entrances to the various rooms.

The Abbot paused to explain.

"The monk's cells are on the second floor. And some community rooms, the laundry, etc. We'll concentrate on the ground level, which is where the work is done."

She turned and led me along the walkway to the first door. The sign above it read:

Day One

She knocked, and a moment later a monk a little older than myself admitted us to a large room with a high ceiling consisting monkstone light panels.

A handful of monks from various orders were at work there. Two bent over a workbench examining something I couldn't identify. Three others sat in a circle before a large monkstone surface, on which were displayed several large diagrams and a jumble of letters (some of them Greek), numbers, and symbols.

"So," I asked, "these monks aren't all from the same order?"

"St. Issac's," the Abbot said, "is an ecumenical monastery. They are, however, all members of the Yerubian Guild—all what you would call 'fleecers.'"

She introduced me to the monk who had admitted us, told him I was a visiting pastor, and asked him to brief me on the work they were doing.

"Don't worry about clearance," she added. "He's cleared much higher than he actually needs to be—for anything you think he might be able to understand, anyway."

They exchanged a knowing smile, and I was a bit embarrassed.

"Please," I said, "Just assume I'm a beginning student at the lowest seminary level, and give me the watered-down version."

He smiled and extended a hand.

"Of course. Welcome."

He waved an arm in a gesture that included the entire room.

"In this division we focus on the first day of creation. As you probably remember, that was day that time was created, and also light, of course. Some of us focus on one, and some on the other. We also work on the relation between the two."

He led me to what looked like an enormous empty aquarium, but was actually a solid, perfectly clear, block of monkstone.

"This is our light-box. It allows us to lay out nearly any fleece we could imagine involving light. For example . . ."

He made a series of complicated gestures, and a ray of light originated at one end of the box, aimed at the other end. About half-way across a disturbance appeared in the clear stone, shaped like the prism I had seen in the Abbot's office. The white light was scattered by this prism, and created a spectrum of colors.

I had, of course, seen this before in a classroom, except with a physical prism that I could have picked up with my hand. But the light box was very impressive.

He gestured again, and the prism disappeared. In its place was a dark plane that stopped the beam completely.

He gestured once more, and two slits appeared in the plane, and a lighter plane appeared further along the light's path. The light played on the second plane with a kind of wave-like pattern.

"So," he said, "you see that pattern? It's like the pattern you'd get if you dropped two stones into the duck pond. The waves would go out evenly until they ran into each other and then you get a pattern like this, when they combined. The light beam is split between the two slits, and when the two beams interact they produce this pattern. The fleece we were laying out when we first did this experiment was asking whether God created light to be more like a wave, or more like an object."

"And the answer was 'more like a wave'?"

"Exactly. If it had been like an object—or like a lot of very tiny objects—then we would have just seen two pools of light on the second surface. But it interacts like a wave."

"Fascinating."

"But there's more. Right now, the box is set up so that we can't tell which slit any particular part of the light is going through. But it can be set up to record that information. And if we do that . . ."

He gestured again, and the light now just made two pools on the second surface. The pattern was completely gone.

"Light is only like a wave if we don't know which slit it is going through. If we do, it's like a lot of little objects. It makes a kind of poetic sense, if you think about it. An object could only go through one slit, but a wave would go through two."

"So which is it?"

He laughed.

"You did ask me to stick to the lowest seminary level. I'm afraid that all I can say at that level is that it seems to be both, but which effect we see depends entirely on which kind of fleece we lay out. If we ask object questions, we get object answers. If we ask wave questions, we get wave answers."

"But you understand it better than what you can explain to an amateur like myself?"

"To some extent, yes. But it's still one of the mysteries of creation."

Chapter 7

"The seeds had been planted earlier, in the late twentieth century—long before the administration of President Caesar Horne set the American democracy wobbling toward its demise—planted with the establishment of a small 'think tank' named the 'Mens Dei Foundation.'"

Lois Bradford, *An Introduction to the Second Enlightenment*

WE VISITED EACH OF THE "DAYS" in turn. The monks in Day Two studied the atmosphere, properties of water, and the general idea of space. The monks in Day Three focused on plants, soil, rocks, and other matters concerning the earth. Day Four was devoted to the moon and stars; Day Five, to birds and fish.

The door to Day Six was opened by a very serious and very slim fellow with very little hair.

He told us that his room was devoted to the study of land animals and human nature.

"Two quite different topics in one room, then," I observed.

"Not so much as you might think. Physically, we *are* animals, after all. We have muscles and bone and brains like they do. We eat and drink and move about in the same ways. And we appear to be descended from animals, as well."

"*Descended* from animals? Isn't that heresy?"

He shared a serious little smile with the Abbot.

"Not heresy. Just deep theology—advanced doctrine. Not the kind of thing that should be shared with laymen, or even the average pastor for that matter."

"Doesn't even 'advanced' doctrine still have to conform to scripture?"

"Of course it does. It just requires a more careful reading than a layperson, or—"

And here he looked meaningfully at me.

"—or a mere pastor, is capable of."

I glared back.

"Try me."

He emitted a dramatic sigh.

"Very well. Think about the whole of the poem that the sixth day occurs in. God creates life—plant life—on day three, yes?"

"Yes."

"And what does plant life create?"

"I'm sorry?"

He rolled his eyes.

"Think!"

I found myself wanting to push his serious little face in.

Instead, I smiled, and tried to remember the exact words from the creation poem.

"Oh. Right. Plants create other plants."

"And how do they do that?"

"By breeding. By producing offspring."

"Like themselves?"

"I believe the phrase is 'after their own kind.'"

"Have you any experience of farming, or gardening?"

"A little."

"So when a plant reproduces 'after its own kind,' does it reproduce an *exact* replica of itself?"

"An approximate replica, I'd say."

"So there are differences?"

"Yes."

"And do these differences accumulate, so that after many different generations a plant might be quite different from it's ancestors?"

"Everyone knows this. It's how we produce varieties that are best for food, or that have the most beautiful blossoms."

"I see you understand. And that same phrase, 'after their kind,' is repeated on day five about the fish and birds?"

"Yes. But what does this have—"

"Patience. We're almost there. And the same is true of the animals created on day six?"

"Okay."

"And we also breed those animals, to change how they look and behave?"

"And?"

"Have you noticed a strange pronoun being used in day six?"

"Not that I recall."

"I'll quote it for you. See if you can spot it. 'And God said let us make humans in our image, after our likeness.'"

He waited, a bit impatiently.

"Well?" he said.

"I suppose you're talking about 'us' and 'our'."

"What do you make of that?"

"One of my professors said it was the 'royal plural,' like the ancient kings would use to refer to themselves."

"That is one possible interpretation. But it tells me that your professor was not privy to deep theology."

"What other interpretation could there be?"

"A much more obvious one. If *you* used the word 'we,' what would that imply?"

"That I was talking about myself and someone else, together."

"Exactly. And who are the others in this verse?"

It finally dawned on me where he had been going all along.

"The *animals?*"

"And what do animals create?"

"Other animals."

"And how do they create them."

"By breeding."

"And human beings are, physically, animals, are we not?"

"But this is just another interpretation—another theory, like my professor's idea of the 'royal plural'."

"Which is why it required a fleece—actually, *many* fleeces —to confirm it."

———

Day Seven turned out to be a room for silent meditation—not a chapel, exactly, though it had that sort of feel. No research went on there, and everyone in the building had access.

The next door wasn't named by a day. It was labeled:

Soul Making

We passed it by. Apparently, it was the only room in the building that required a higher access than I had been given.

After passing that door, the Abbot took me to a bench on the covered walkway.

"We have one more room to visit, but before we do I wondered if you have any questions about what you've seen already."

"I do have a kind of background question. It's about the whole idea of fleecing."

She chuckled.

"Let me guess. You're wondering if it doesn't contradict Joshua's teaching about not testing God."

My mouth must have dropped open at that, because she shook her head a little and continued.

"I can't read minds. But I get asked that question almost every time I meet a Fundamentalist pastor."

"And the answer is?"

"The short answer is 'No,' but I suspect you want a little more than that. It comes down to context. Why does that make you smile?"

"I had a . . . a *friend* once, who used to argue theology with me. She was a great believer in context."

"I see. Well, in this case the question is what the word 'test' means, in context. When Joshua used it the question was whether he should force God to prove his integrity by arbitrarily putting himself in danger. He refused, quite rightly. But do you know the story of Yeruba'al?

"Of course. An angel or God himself—it's not exactly clear from the text—commands Yeruba'al to lead an army into battle, and promises him victory. Yeruba'al asks for a sign as proof."

"Proof that God will keep his word?"

"No. Proof that it's really God speaking to him. So he builds an altar, and the angel holds out a staff and sets the sacrifice on fire."

"And does this convince Yeruba'al?"

"At first it seems to, but then later he asks for more proof."

"Put yourself in Yeruba'al's place. Why wasn't the first sign good enough?"

I thought about that before replying.

"He requested that sign to prove that this was really a message from God. But the sign itself was chosen by the angel, which meant it could have been a trick of some kind. The 'angel' could have been an enemy posing as a messenger from God, or a demon or something, and the trick with the staff wouldn't disprove that."

"Very good. So why did he do what he did next?"

"Oh. I see. He put a sheepskin—a fleece—out overnight, then asked as a sign that it would be wet in the morning and the ground around it would be dry. The next night he did the same, but asked the opposite—that the skin would be dry in the morning, but the ground wet."

"And why was that sign better than the trick with the staff?"

"Because Yeruba'al chose it himself. The 'angel,' if it wasn't an angel, couldn't just use whatever trick he already had up his sleeve. And because it involved a real miracle. Only God could cause an event that went directly against nature. And also because he reversed it on the second night. So that if there were some natural way that it could happen, that wouldn't explain a completely opposite event the second time."

"Exactly. And that's the difference between the 'test' that Joshua refused, and the 'test' that Yeruba'al performed. Joshua refused to test God's integrity. Yeruba'al was testing whether the message he was getting was truly from God."

"But I still don't see how that applies to the work fleecers do here."

"We aren't testing in either of those senses, exactly. But what we do is like Yeruba'al's fleece, in that he was trying to determine the *truth* of the matter. So he created a fleece which couldn't be influenced by his own interpretation, or be 'answered' by a mere coincidence or a trick.

"We are striving to learn the truth of God's creation—and by extension, of its creator—so we strive to create fleeces like Yeruba'al—fleeces that aren't open to misinterpretation."

"I see. At least I think I do. I'd like to talk some more about this after I give it some thought."

"I'll be happy to."

It was getting chilly on that bench.

"So what's next?

"The final stop on our tour. I left it to last because I think you'll want to spend some time there. The monk I'm going to introduce you to is the person I told you about yesterday afternoon—who I thought might be able to help with your spiritual problem. He's agreed to try."

"I'm very grateful."

"I should warn you. He's a bit eccentric. His methods will probably be unorthodox, even opaque. But if you're patient, I think he'll help you in the end."

"That's a very intriguing endorsement."

"Yes, well, you'll soon see."

Chapter 8

THE SIGN on the last door read:

MASTER WRIGHT

It was locked like the others, but this time the Abbot gestured at the entry plate, and pulled on the handle.

I was curious.

"Is this *your* workshop as well?"

"I'm the only qualified substitute, in case the Master Wright falls ill, so I have access."

The first thing I saw as we entered was eerily familiar.

It was a large round table, its surface a dull black liquid. It was topped by an equally large transparent dome—one which I knew, from experience, I could have put my hand right through without any resistance at all.

I had caught a glimpse of a much smaller one at seminary—through an open door to a room where I wasn't allowed. But I had seen one almost this size once, as well. And that had been in the workroom of a sorcerer.

It was a creation chamber or, as the sorcerer had informed me, a 'firmament.'

It stood just in front of the door as we entered, and directly across from us, on the other side of it, stood the tall monk I had seen as I arrived the day before.

He was even taller than I remembered. If I'd been asked to guess his age, I would have put him in his late fifties or early sixties. His skin was darker than mine, though not as dark as Dennis', and his long head was topped with an unruly—and probably never combed—mop of hair. His eyes, a penetrating blue, set off an enormous nose. The logo over his left eyebrow was the same as my own—the triple *F* of the Fellowship of Free Fundamentalists.

He stood behind a slender stand, which came up to the level of his waist and held a small tray containing what appeared to be a single coin. His robe was belted with a metal chain.

At the center of the firmament between us, emerging from the dark liquid on its surface, was what appeared to be a golden bug, as large as the palm of my hand.

He made a gesture of the same sort I had once witnessed

the sorcerer using, and the bug abruptly stopped rising from the liquid.

He made a second gesture, and it descended again until it was swallowed whole.

Then he turned his attention our way, and granted me a self-deprecating grin.

"Can't always get it right on the first try, I'm afraid."

He wrinkled his brow, then laughed.

"Or, in this case, on the fifth or sixth."

He addressed the Abbot.

"Is this our young pastor, then?"

She nodded.

"Well, come on in—the water's fine."

We made our way around the firmament into the center of his workshop.

It was an amazing clutter.

There were several worktables, one littered with pencils and papers covered with all kinds of sketches and diagrams and even writing and numbers—the kind of thing most people would keep in their Bibles.

Another table held an array of objects I couldn't guess the purpose of—but I had come to expect that after seeing the Abbot's office.

Still another held a variety of coin-shaped pieces of what appeared to be metal—like the one which I had seen when we entered, on the tray in front of the monk. Each of these had a combination of words, numbers, and symbols etched into its surface. On one end of the table stood a stack of similar coins with blank surfaces.

The walls were covered with a variety of shelves, each also containing a few objects I could identify, but many more that I couldn't. They weren't stored in an orderly fashion like those in the Abbot's office, but jammed together in a fantastic disorder, some piled on others, some tilted on an edge, some seemingly ready to come tumbling down at any moment.

There was a modest camp-bed in one corner, and a slanted drawing board in another.

A third corner held his altar, and a large coffee pot. Empty and half-empty cups stood on every work table. The aroma of coffee permeated the room.

Our host stuck out a large wrinkled hand.

"Macon Chavez, Master Wright, at your service."

"Adam Kinde. Thank you for agreeing to counsel me."

"If you don't mind," said the Abbot, "I would like to complete Adam's tour before we get to his spiritual problem. Then I can leave the two of you to talk."

So Brother Macon showed us around his domain. Aside from the clutter, it was similar to the sorcerer's workshop that I had already seen. The central feature was the firmament—the round table we had first seen when we entered. It was capable of creating almost anything the monk could design. And it was essential to the entire facility, since most of the tools I had witnessed on my tour—the light box in Day One, for example— had been created using it.

The coin-like disks I had seen each stored the word for one of his creations. When one was put on the tray, it controlled the process that produced that particular object.

Brother Macon had had a long career as a fleecer himself before retiring to his post as Master Wright. The Abbot hinted that he had been something of a genius, with a rather colorful history in fleecer circles. He didn't seem to want to discuss why he had left that work for this humble role, so I didn't pry.

When he had finished showing us around, the Abbot said goodbye and turned to leave. But she paused and turned halfway out of the door.

"Oh, Pastor. Your friend, Sister Edith, has persuaded me to

give her a throwing demonstration after all. We're meeting at my office after lunch. Would you care to join us?"

"I'll look forward to it."

"Good. I'll see you then."

She closed the door behind her, and Brother Macon turned his attention to me.

"So you know Sister Edith?"

"Yes and no. I knew her before she was Sister Edith. From my seminary days."

"I see."

He raised one eyebrow at me.

"And you are experiencing an absence of God?"

"I am."

"Exactly."

He dragged a short wooden stool across the room, climbed up on it, and reached something down from a top shelf. When he turned around, I could see that he held—of all things—a well-worn deck of Shadow cards. He spread them, face up, before me.

"Choose a card, but don't touch it, and don't tell me what it is until I ask."

"I don't understand. Is this part of my—"

"Choose a card. Don't touch it. Don't say what it is."

I looked back down at the deck.

"Okay."

"You will remember it?"

"Yes."

He scooped up the cards, put them back in their box, and returned them to their shelf.

"You still remember the card?"

"Yes."

"What was it?"

"The *M* of hearts."

He gave a nod of satisfaction.

"You see the box on the table behind you?"

I turned around.

"Yes."

"Pick it up."

I did as he asked. There was a folded piece of drawing paper beneath it.

"Now," he said, "Pick up that paper."

I picked up the paper.

"Unfold it."

There was a sketch inside—of a Shadow card. The *M* of hearts.

"That's a very good trick, but I don't see what it has to do with—"

"Do you find the trick puzzling?"

"Of course."

"Why?"

"Well, because—I suppose because you had to have drawn that sketch before I chose the card, so you couldn't have known which card I was going to choose when you drew it."

"Very good. Now unpack that."

"Unpack it?"

"Yes. What assumptions were you making in that description."

"Assumptions? Well, I assumed that you drew the sketch before I saw it. . ."

"And why did you assume that?"

"Because that's how time works."

"Not quite. Try again."

"Because that's . . . that's how time works in my experience?"

"Close enough. You'll do better, later. What else?"

I tried to remember what I had said.

"I assumed that you couldn't have known which card I was going to pick—unless!"

"Yes?"

"Unless there was some way you *could* know. Some way of making me choose the card you wanted. Maybe something in the way you spread out the cards, or . . . "

"Very good. We have made a start. I think we'll stop for now, and begin in earnest tomorrow morning, after breakfast."

He nodded toward the door.

I shook his hand and made my way out, but he called to me before the door closed.

"Would you do a favor for me this afternoon?"

I grabbed the handle to keep the door open.

"If I can."

"Tell Sister Edith that Brother Macon sends his greetings."

Chapter 9

"Two honest observers peer into a fishbowl from opposite sides. One speaks only the language of science, the other only the language of religion. They describe the same fish, and their descriptions are absolutely at odds. Should they fight to the death over their differences? Or cooperate to build a third and better language?"

Ram Jacobs, Senior Fellow, Mens Dei, *Prolegomena to an Integrated Worldview*

WHEN I APPROACHED the Abbot's door after lunch, Lilith was already there, waiting for me. She threw her arms around me and kissed my cheek.

I wasn't sure how I felt about that.

"Adam," she gushed. "It's so good to see you again. We must find time to catch up while I'm here."

"That would be nice. If I can. I'm really here on presbytery business, so . . ."

"You'll be able to find a little time. I'll make sure of it."

I changed the subject by delivering Brother Macon's message.

She seemed pleased.

"How sweet. Will you be seeing him again?"

"Fairly often while I'm here, it seems."

"Then give him my good wishes . . ."

She paused, considering, then continued.

". . . and could you tell him that if we are going to exchange gifts, we might have to do it early, because I may need to leave before Resurrection Morning?"

"Sure."

"In fact, if you wouldn't mind, could you tell him that I'll send my gift with you when I get a chance?"

Before we could knock, the Abbot opened her door and joined us. She led us along the porch, then through the garden to the other end of the Abbey.

Lilith walked next to me, a bit closer than I would have liked.

Our path passed through a gap in a high hedge which encircled a large open clearing. Inside, next to the entrance, stood a small storage shed. At the far end, a wooden target about four feet across stood between two trees.

The sky overhead was cloudless and blue, but the air was still bitterly cold.

The Abbot opened the door of the shed to reveal an array of throwing knives hanging on the back wall, which was only about six inches away. They all looked similar to the one that hung on the wall of her office, except that they weren't gold-plated.

She removed three of them, closed the shed, and turned to Lilith.

"I'm not sure how you talked me into this. I haven't thrown with an audience for twenty years, at least."

Lilith just smiled.

"I'm honored—*we're* honored."

The Abbot transferred one of the knives to her throwing hand, cocked an eye at the target, pulled her arm back, and threw.

I had always thought that a thrown knife had to rotate end over end on its way to the target, but this one didn't. It went straight as an arrow, and stuck firmly in the bullseye.

The other two knives followed in quick succession, so that the three blades actually touched each other at the center of the target.

Lilith gave a low whistle.

"Amazing!"

The Abbot turned to me.

"Would you mind retrieving the blades?"

I walked to the target and, with some effort, wrenched the knives out of the bullseye. They had gone deep into the wood, and it took me a moment to dislodge them. The Abbot had a surprisingly powerful arm.

When I returned, she was already instructing Lilith on throwing technique. She took the knives from me, and demonstrated the correct grip, the angle to pull the arm back at, and how to release the blade.

When she finished, she motioned for me to stand well back, out of the way, and nodded for Lilith to throw.

Lilith's brow furrowed with concentration, and her tongue stuck out of the corner of her mouth as she made her first throw, which stuck firmly in the trunk of the tree to the left of the target.

She gave a disappointed sigh, and tried again.

Her second blade stuck in a branch of the tree at the right—about a foot higher than the top of the target.

Her third try stuck in one leg of the stand which held the target.

She surveyed her failures with her hands on her hips.

"Well," she said, "that was a lot harder than I expected."

"Actually, you did quite well. Many amateurs can't even make the knife stick at first."

Lilith shrugged.

"Beginner's luck, I suspect."

"Shall we ask Pastor Kinde to retrieve your blades?"

"No. I threw them. I'll bring them back."

"And Pastor, did you want a turn?"

"Thank you, but I'm happy to remain a spectator."

"Then I have to get back to the office. Could you come with me? We can chat on the way. There's a cloth in the shed, Sister Edith, to dry the knives with before hanging them back up. Be sure to close the door tightly."

The Abbot waited until we were out of earshot before speaking.

"Forgive me for asking this, but when you knew Sister Edith before, would you say she was a *transparent* person?"

"Transparent?"

"As opposed, I suppose, to deceitful?"

"I'm not sure—"

"Was she the kind of person who would intentionally mislead others?"

"I don't think so. Why?"

"It's just . . . She's *very* good at knife throwing."

"She missed every time."

"She didn't hit the target. But she hit exactly what she was aiming at. A complete amateur wouldn't have got all three knives to stick at that distance, even if they actually hit anything. An amateur wouldn't even have hit something all three times. But aside from that, her form was perfect, though she went to great lengths to make it look like it wasn't."

"Why would she?"

"I'm not sure. Perhaps to flatter me, by making me look better."

"That would seem to be unnecessary."

She shot a smile at me.

"Nicely said. But if she's as good as I think she is, she could have made my performance appear quite ordinary. And I suppose that *could* explain it. She may just be unwilling to embarrass her host."

She changed the subject.

"So, did yesterday's tour help you with your 'fact-finding' mission?"

"Actually it was quite helpful."

"I can't imagine how. In spite of your high access, I don't think you learned a thing that you couldn't have picked up in seminary."

"I would say that 'Day Six' was quite a revelation."

"I suppose. Did that help you with your mission?"

"Not really."

"So what did?"

I didn't answer.

We reached building, and stepped up onto the end of the porch. Her wind chimes tinkled softly ahead of us.

"What about your counseling session with Brother Macon, then?"

"That's harder to say. It was short—and perplexing."

She smiled.

"I warned you."

Then she became more serious.

"Please give him a chance. His methods tend to be . . . well, rather inscrutable, I know. But if you stick it out, I think you'll be glad you did."

"I'll stick it out."

"Good. What you're going through can't be pleasant."

Chapter 10

"We are engaged in a war between the Godless discipline of science and the holy mission of the church. We will never win by pushing the enemy back. We must invade his territory; we must conquer it and subjugate it. We must create a world in which all knowledge is the property of the church."

Timothy Bentwater, Senior Fellow, Mens Dei, *Queen of the Sciences: The Battle for the Human Mind*

THE NEXT MORNING Brother Earnest approached me after breakfast and offered to escort me to my meeting with Brother Macon.

I agreed and thanked him, though I wasn't likely to get lost on the way. It occurred to me that perhaps the Abbot didn't trust me as much as she claimed.

But about two-thirds of the way there, I realized the real reason, which was merely pragmatic. Someone had to let me into the building.

"So," I said, "you have access to the research facility? I thought you were the guest master?

Brother Earnest shot me another of his broad smiles.

"It's only one of my many hats. I'm the Abbot's direct assistant, so I have access pretty much everywhere she does."

He went in with me, and opened the door to Brother Macon's lair as well before leaving me.

Brother Macon was seated at the large drawing board in one corner, working on a sketch. He spoke without turning around.

"Come in, Pastor! Find a seat. Would you like some coffee? I think there's a clean cup by the pot."

There was indeed one clean cup sitting by the pot, which I considered to be something of a miracle in that room. I filled it with coffee and found a chair.

After a moment, he turned around and settled his eyes on me.

"I think we had best begin with your catechism. *What is the Holy Duality?*"

I recited the answer I had been made to memorize at seminary.

"*The Holy Duality is the central mystery of our faith. The Word of God is God, and the Spirit of God is God. The Word is not the Spirit and the Spirit is not the Word, but where the Word is, there is Spirit, and where the Spirit is there is Word.*"

"And do you understand what you just said?"

"It can't be understood. It's a mystery."

"Hmm. And when you say it *can't* be understood, do you mean that it is impossible to understand, or that it would be a *sin* to understand it?"

"The first one. It's impossible, not *wrong*. People are always trying. One professor said it was like ice and steam—ice isn't steam, and steam isn't ice, but they're both water. But that doesn't fit, really, because you can have ice without having steam, and steam without ice."

"Yes. Material analogies tend to be very popular in seminaries. Ironic. Here's another."

He rummaged through a box on the worktable nearest him, and finally came up with a metal loop, which he handed to me.

The metal was flat with rounded edges so that it had two sides. But the loop had a twist in it, so that one side became the other as it went around.

"It's called a Duality loop. You see the analogy? Every point on the loop has two sides, yet if you follow either side around the loop, it becomes the other side. So the two are one. It's a nice sort of symbol of the Duality, but as an explanation it falls as flat as the ice and water analogy."

"But *you* really like it."

He raised an eyebrow.

"What makes you say that?"

"Your belt."

He glanced down at the chain around his waist. It was made up of links like the loop I held in my hand.

"I do have a fondness for the shape, even though it doesn't quite do its job. But back to your catechism. You agree that there's no sin in trying to understand the Duality?"

Suddenly I wasn't so sure about that.

"I guess no sin. But of course no point as well, since the catechism tells us it's impossible."

"And suppose that the catechism was mistaken on that point?"

"How could the catechism be mistaken?"

"It's not scripture, after all. Suppose that it *did* turn out to be possible to understand the Duality. Would you want to try?"

He had me there. There has never been a mystery I didn't want to solve.

On the other hand, I had the feeling that I was being drawn in to something approaching heresy. But—on the third hand, I suppose—wasn't I there precisely for that purpose: to sniff out heresy?

I took a deep breath.

"Yes. Of course. Who wouldn't?"

"Are those two terms—'word' and 'spirit'—applied only to God in the scriptures?"

"No. They're also applied to humans."

"So humans have a sort of duality as well?"

"Possibly."

"Now where do you think the ancients got this idea—of human duality?"

"I don't know."

"Might the terms themselves be a clue?"

"The terms?"

"'Word' and 'spirit.' What do those terms mean?"

"Well, 'spirit' was another word for breath or wind."

"Not just 'air,' then?"

"No. It was the movement."

"The energy?"

"That makes sense."

"And if 'spirit' is the energy of breath, what would 'word' be?"

I suddenly realized where he was headed.

"It's an analogy to speech, isn't it? The thing that turns the energy of the breath into speech is the *shaping* of the breath, the articulation in the mouth, that gives it structure!"

"So the word—the structure, the articulation—is not the

spirit—the breath, the energy—and yet, in the act of speech you can't have one without the other."

"Not if you have speech."

"Is that more satisfactory than the analogy of ice and steam?"

"I think so—possibly."

"Or the links in my belt?"

"Definitely."

"And if you were to search the scriptures, you would find this analogy applied to ordinary people—and specifically to their acts. Have you ever been in love?"

It caught me off-guard. A vision of monkstone light on bare metal surfaced in my mind, and I forced it back down.

Brother Macon put a hand on my shoulder.

"Are you all right?"

"Sorry. You jogged a painful memory."

"I didn't mean to."

"It's . . . It's okay. I just got taken by surprise, and the memory is still—still pretty raw."

"Do you want to go on?"

"Can we use another example?"

"How about a different time—a different woman. It doesn't have to be your truest love."

Lilith, then.

I took a breath.

"Okay. I have someone else in mind."

"Then think about a time when you did something for her —gave her a gift, perhaps. Some act of lo—of affection."

"I gave her a bouquet of flowers once."

"That will do nicely. So how did you come by these flowers?"

"We had passed a field on one of our walks, and I notice how much they pleased her. Her birthday was coming up, so I went back to the field and picked them and brought them home. I had bought a pretty little vase in town, and I arranged them nicely, then put them on the table where she would see them the moment she entered."

"So the structure, the articulation, the 'word' of that act was what?"

"Everything I just said, from noticing which flowers she liked, to gathering them, arranging them—all of it."

"And what would you say the energy was, that empowered that act?"

"How I felt about her—affection. I suppose at the time I would have said 'love'."

"And the content of the act?"

"Also love."

"So the spirit is both the content and the energy of the act, and the word is the structure of the act?"

"That does seem right."

"Would you have done all this without the spirit—without the affection you had for this person?"

"I wouldn't have."

"And would this act have existed without the word—without the form and structure that all your planning and actions gave to that spirit?"

"No."

"So the act was both spirit and word?"

"Yes."

"But the word was not spirit, and the spirit was not word?"

"Yes."

"And would you call what you did for her 'creative'?"

"Definitely."

"Would you say that one distinction between humans and the other animals is that we are more creative?"

"How do you mean?"

"Do other animals arrange flowers for their partners, or cook their meals differently all the time, or paint paintings in multiple styles, or create various kinds of music?"

"I never thought of that. We are creators. We are creative about almost everything we do."

"And every act of creation is an act of word and spirit?"

"Fascinating."

"Do you remember what the Book of Beginnings says about the creation of humans, on the sixth day?"

"It says we were created in God's image."

"And in the context of that passage, what do we know about God?"

I laughed.

"Context again."

"I'm sorry?"

"Never mind. The passage is about God creating everything, through his word and spirit."

"So is it surprising that if we are created in his image, that we would also create through word and spirit?"

"But . . . but why didn't they teach me this in seminary?"

* * *

I DECIDED to go for a walk after leaving the research facility, so I followed the path until it neared the pond, then cut across the snow to the trail that led to the cemetery.

Brother Macon hadn't given me a satisfactory answer to my question. His analogy had made sense, and was backed by the scriptures—so why hadn't I learned it in my seminary training? For that matter, why did the catechism we all memorized go to such great lengths to hide the truth?

I didn't have an answer for that.

And I didn't have the slightest idea why Brother Macon

thought that an arcane theological analogy had anything to do with my very real spiritual problem. Understanding the Holy Duality was certainly interesting, but I couldn't see how it helped me deal with being abandoned by God.

I reached the trail and realized my mistake. My feet were freezing. Living in the warmth of the San Fernando Valley, I hadn't come equipped to wade through snow in freezing temperatures.

I almost turned back, but decided that the exercise might warm me if I kept going.

It was possible, of course, that I was getting some insight into what Brother Macon's heresy might be. But that didn't make me feel any better. Brine's heresy hunt was getting more distasteful by the moment.

My two suspects—Macon and the Abbot—were good people, as far as I could see. What harm did it do if they weren't perfectly orthodox? As I had pointed out to Brine on that wet bench, wasn't everyone a heretic on some point?

The idea of using my friendship—using their efforts to help me—to catch them out and turn them in . . .

I came to the split in the trail, one part winding up toward the cemetery, the other down to the hermitage.

I stopped there, watching for the hermit.

Another unanswered question—why had Brine warned me away from the hermit?

I stood there as long as my feet could tolerate it, occasionally stomping the ground to warm them up, but there was no activity, nothing to see.

I had intended to hike all the way to the cemetery, but my feet disagreed.

I headed back toward the warmth of my room.

I wondered what Lucky was doing.

Had he gone, or stayed?

I needed to get back home, to deal with that.

I needed to continue my search for Aunt Joan.

But I also needed to follow my orders.

And I needed to understand what role Lilith played in all of this.

Because she did.

Brother Macon's lessons on the Holy Duality had at least made me certain of that.

Chapter 11

"Resonance is the essence of true creation. Resonance between a painting and its reference, between the art and the artist, between the image and its source."

Brother Macon Chavez

AFTER LUNCH I warmed my feet by the fire in the common room for a while, then went back to my room. I wanted to make some notes in my Bible, and try to sort out what my next steps were.

While I had caught a whiff of heresy—or something very like it—from Brother Macon, I had made no progress on the Abbot. As much as I wanted her to be innocent, it was my duty to try, so I would need to contrive more time with her.

And while Lilith was not part of my original mission, I was sure she was involved after what I had learned in my last session with Macon. So I needed to arrange more time with her, as well.

There was a knock on my door.

I opened it to find Lilith standing outside, shivering.

"Can I come in?"

"I'm not sure we're allowed to—"

"Adam! I'm freezing."

I backed away to let her in. She closed the door behind her.

"I think the temperature's dropped another ten degrees."

"Yeah. It's cold enough. You're here because . . .?"

"We haven't had that chance to catch up yet. I went down to the common room to find you, but they said you'd headed up here."

I offered her the chair and sat myself on the edge of the bed.

"So," I said, "You're a Joshuan now."

"I joined a month after we broke up. Do you still make a mean omelet?"

"I've gotten better, actually. And the thing with what's-his-name—"

"Samael."

"The thing with Samael didn't last?"

"It lasted. Samael wasn't a boyfriend. I just let you think that. It was easier."

"Who was he, then?"

"A sort of spiritual counselor, with the Joshuans. I had decided to take my vows. Did I break your heart?"

"For a while."

"I'm sorry about that. So. Tell me about you. You're a pastor now."

"Back in the village on the Franklyn estate, where I grew up."

"And married?"

"No."

"Really? I thought I detected the extra reserve of a married man."

"I was *almost* married. She's gone, but I'm not—"

"Not over her."

"It wasn't that long ago."

So I told her about Bee. She listened, and as my story unfolded my defenses dropped. I even came close—but only close—to tears at one point.

After that the conversation wandered toward old times. We laughed at old stories, she remembered the time I picked those flowers for her, we wondered what had happened to some of our friends.

In the end I felt I was talking to the old Lilith—the one I had known before the breakup—and it was good.

It was so good that I almost forgot to ask the questions I had planned on. I don't think I would have remembered if she hadn't broken the spell.

"Before I forget," she said, "did you give my message to Brother Macon?"

"I did. And he said he had a gift for you, as well."

"Thanks. I'll dig mine out, so I can send it with you."

"Where do you know him from?"

"We met at an ecumenical conference last year. We were on the same committee."

"But you didn't know the *Abbot* before you came here?"

"She didn't go to that conference. Why?"

"Just getting everyone straight in my head. All the relation-ships. It seemed unusual, that you would know Brother Macon —given how little Joshuans get about."

"I suppose."

I took a chance.

"I've never met one before—a Joshuan. I didn't even know what style of stones you wore."

She grinned, and lifted her wrist, so I could see it better.

"What do you think?"

"Very stylish. It's an unusual bracelet, too. Do all Joshuans wear that style of chain?"

"Some do. Not all."

Supper was poached salmon with asparagus. Monks seemed to eat very well.

I caught the Abbot after the evening meal, and scheduled an appointment the following afternoon. Then I lingered in the common room for an hour or so, restless, as though I was waiting for something. I wasn't sure what.

Finally I headed back to my room and read myself to sleep.

The next morning after breakfast Brother Earnest escorted me back to the research facility, and I had another session with Brother Macon.

"Who do you believe created the world you live in?"

I was sitting on the same stool I had chosen the day before, but he was standing this time—a bit too close for comfort, so I had to tilt my head back to look up at his long head and enormous nose.

The coffee-pot was making coffee-pot noises in the corner.

I thought it was an odd question for him to ask.

"God created it, of course."

"So you believe you live in the world that God created, then?"

"What other world is there?"

"Very good. That is an appropriate question. How would you answer it?"

"It was a rhetorical question. The answer is 'none.'"

"Hmm."

He rolled up the sleeves of his robe so that his forearms were bare. He then selected one of the blank disks from his workbench, and held it by the edges between his thumb and forefinger for my inspection.

"What am I holding?"

"A disk. One of those disks that control the firmament."

He didn't respond, so I elaborated.

"It hasn't got any writing on it, so I assume it's a blank disk —one that hasn't been used yet."

He finally nodded.

"Better. And this disk is in the world you live in?"

"It's right in front of me."

"And the hand that is holding it, as well?"

"Of course."

He held up his left hand, spread his fingers out, and turned it back and front.

"And this hand. It is also in your world?"

"Yes."

"And it is empty in your world?"

"It is."

He very slowly took the disk from his right hand, keeping the whole process in my view. Then he spread the fingers of that hand in the same way and turned it back and front.

"And this hand is also empty in your world?"

"Absolutely."

He held the the disk facing me in his left hand, and moved his right hand between it and me, hiding it for just a fraction of a second. When his left hand came into view again there were *two* disks facing me: one between his thumb and forefinger and the other between his forefinger and middle finger.

"And how many disks are there in your world, now?"

It was a good trick. I laughed.

"Two."

He passed his hand in front of the disks again, and there was only one.

"And now?"

"One again."

He finally sat down, so I didn't have to crane my neck. He granted me a sheepish smile.

"I admit, I'm tempted to show you some more tricks, but this is enough for our present purpose. In your world, there was one coin, which magically became two, then magically became one again. Do you believe that is what happened in God's world?"

"But it was just a trick, right?"

"That word is often misleading."

"Trick?"

"No. 'Just'. When you find yourself using that word you should always be suspicious—you should ask yourself what truth you are trying to avoid."

I didn't have anything to say to that. So I waited, and he continued.

"You're right that it was a trick, but that doesn't change the lesson the trick is teaching. Can you see the difference—even if it's 'just' a trick—between what happened in *your* world, and what happened in *God's* world?"

"I can see that there must *be* a difference."

This amused him. He nodded and handed me the disk.

I turned it over in my hand, and after a moment I realized that it had never been what I had thought. Rather than a single solid disk, it was a solid disk covered with a thin shell, like a disk-shaped container.

He took it back, and showed me the way he had separated

the disk from its shell—which, if you only saw one side, looked exactly like a second disk.

"So," he said, "in God's world there was a disk in a shell. And in your world—the world you live in—there was a single disk, then two disks, then a single disk again."

"I think I see."

"And who created your world? Who saw a solid disk instead of one side of an empty shell?"

"I did."

"Yes, you did. We all do, all the time. Sometimes the world we create, and live in, is like God's world, and sometimes it's different. But even when it's the same, we have to create it in order to live in it."

He plopped the disk out of its shell into my hand, then closed my fingers around it.

"A spiritual exercise. Put this in your pocket. Carry it wherever you go. Whenever you touch it or see it, remind yourself that you are the creator of the world you live in, that only you can keep it from being a false world."

He stood and pulled a small package from one of his shelves. It was tied with a ribbon.

"And this is my gift for Sister Edith. Thank you for giving it to her."

Chapter 12

"Ram Jacobs' insistence that the concept of 'fleecing' be based on a scriptural model may seem naïve to the contemporary reader, but it was both honest and powerful in its historical context."

Rita Willnard, *Mens Dei and the Tribulation Crisis*

THE ABBOT WAS POURING tea as I entered her office. She passed me a cup, and took a sip of her own.

"So is this about your 'mission,' or about your sessions with Brother Macon?"

I just needed to get her talking. The subject didn't really matter.

"You had promised to tell me a bit more about fleecing."

"I'd forgotten about that. What would you like to know?"

"I'm not sure. I don't know enough yet to know what I don't know, if that makes sense."

"So you need some kind of overview—fleecing 101?"

"I suppose so."

"All right. Let's see. The first thing to say, I guess, is that fleecing is a *spiritual* discipline above all else."

"A spiritual discipline?"

"Let's go back to the story of Yeruba'al. He laid that fleece out—twice—in order to be certain that he was hearing the voice of God. Why do you think he was so cautious, so careful?"

"He thought the angel might be lying."

"That's true, but there's something else that he was even more afraid of."

"What was that?"

"If the angel *was* lying, what had to happen for that lie to be successful?"

I was silent.

She waited.

And then it clicked.

"He'd have to *believe* the lie."

"Exactly. And the spiritual danger was that the angel was telling him something that he *wanted* to be true—that he was going to be a mighty warrior and lead his people to victory."

"And he was afraid that he, himself, would be too easy to convince."

"The first thing every fleecer learns is that we must constantly be on guard against believing the thing that we *want* to believe."

She opened a drawer and pulled out a drawing.

"I have a much better example than this one, but it's not here, so I'll show it to you another time."

She pushed the drawing toward me.

· · ·

"WHAT DO YOU SEE."

"It's a cartoon of a duck."

She shook her head.

"Look harder. It's a rabbit."

I stared at it.

"I only see a duck."

"Keep trying."

I stared some more.

"Wait! I see it now. Very clever. It depends on how I look at it."

"It actually *does*. I know you meant that as a sort of figure of speech, but it literally does depend on *how* you look. If you focus your eyes a little below and to the left of the dot, you'll see the duck."

"You're right! I do."

"And if you focus a little above the dot and to the right, the bump becomes a nose, and you'll see—"

"The rabbit! If I focus there, I can't see the duck. And if I force myself to see the duck my focus moves back to the other spot."

"The point is that how we look at something changes what we see."

"Like seeing light as waves, or as little objects?"

"Well, not exactly. The shift in the word of light from wave forms to object forms actually happens in the light box. The shift from duck to rabbit only happens in your mind."

"I get it. Waves or objects exist in God's world, while ducks and rabbits exist in my world?"

"So Macon's taking you down *that* road. What else has he taught you, I wonder?"

She paused for a moment, weighing me with her eyes, then continued.

"But to stick to the present point, if it were really important to you to see the duck and *not* to see the rabbit, you might very well find it impossible to see the rabbit at all."

"And fleecers are often tempted in this way?"

"Constantly. Our job is to stare at creation, and try to see the patterns—to see the word of the creator at work. We lay out fleeces to help us do that. But which fleeces we lay out, and how we interpret them, can change what we see."

"And there are some things you may not want to see."

"Our reputations and self-respect can get all tangled up in the patterns we see. So if we've been working on a duck pattern for years, and someone else suggests a rabbit pattern, we can be very resistant to seeing the rabbit."

"And that's how it's a spiritual problem."

"Exactly. I'll tell you more about this when I've brought that other example to the office, if you like."

"I would."

I stood to leave.

"But," I said, "before I go, can I ask you something about Brother Macon? Two things, actually."

"Of course."

"I'm finding his approach a bit confusing, partly because it seems to border on heresy at times."

"That doesn't *sound* like a question."

"Am I wrong? Or is he a bit of a heretic?"

"Is this part of your 'fact-finding'?"

"Am I? Wrong?"

She stared me down.

"And your second question?"

"My second question is more mundane. I noticed that the links in your necklace and the links in his belt were similar, and quite unusual. I was wondering why."

"We're old friends, and one of Macon's hobbies is metalwork. We have a workshop for that, here. He designed his belt, and he made me this chain as a gift."

"It's just that—that you never met Sister Edith before she came here on Monday, right?"

"Where exactly is this going?"

"I noticed that her bracelet has the same style of links. But I suppose if Brother Macon gives them out to friends . . ."

"Yes, that would explain it."

"Well. Thank you for taking the time to instruct me."

"No problem at all. In fact, I find myself wondering if Brother Macon is going to be able to give you all the help you need."

"I'm willing to keep trying."

"I'm sure. But I think I'd like to have someone else see you as well. Just as a sort of supplement to Brother Macon's efforts."

ON THE WAY back to my room I saw Lilith going into hers. I remembered the gift from Brother Macon, so I went to my room and retrieved it.

The word on her door was "Chastity". I knocked. When she opened it, she was pulling her robe closed. Not quite quickly enough.

She blushed.

"Sorry," she said. "I wasn't expecting anyone."

"I'm not offended."

"Well, it's not like you've never seen them before."

Then she realized what I was staring at.

She stepped back and her hand jumped to cover her forehead.

"I've seen that before," I said, "as well."

She brought her hand down.

"Odd. This makes me feel more naked than the other. But of course you're right."

"So you kept your old logo? Joshuans allow that?"

"We all keep them. Other orders require members to leave their past behind them. We bring all we are to the order—including our past. It's why we always wear the headbands in public."

I held out the little box.

"Brother Macon's Resurrection gift."

"Oh. Thank you. Can I give you my gift for him?"

She retreated into the room, calling over her shoulder.

"Don't leave the door open. Come on in."

I stepped just inside, closing the door behind me. Her room was as tidy as my own, everything in its place. But there was something about it that stirred a memory. Something I couldn't identify.

She had tossed Brother Macon's gift on the bed, and knelt with her back to me to open her suitcase.

"Have a seat. I won't be a moment."

I sat in the only chair and let my eyes roam the room, trying to put my finger on what I was remembering. But aside from a different suitcase and a few items on the dresser it was remarkably like my own room.

There was, of course, her figure bent over the suitcase, her bare feet protruding from under her robe. That was familiar enough even though the clothes were different.

But that wasn't it.

"Got it!"

She beamed at me, holding up a box very much like the one on the bed, and then I realized.

Her perfume. I hadn't noticed it before—not even the other night in my own room—but it was quite strong here in her room, and quite what I remembered.

I stood, and she crossed the room to hand me the gift. As she put it into my hand she leaned forward and kissed me on the cheek—for the second time.

"Thanks for doing this."

"Glad to help."

"And thanks for not minding about . . . You're a dear."

I WAS COMPLETELY LOST in something vaguely resembling thought on my way back to my own room, and so I didn't notice the Abbot coming toward me until she spoke.

"Pastor?"

I came out of my trance to see her standing in front of me.

"Oh. Hello."

"Are you all right?"

It took me a second to process the question.

"Yes. I'm fine. Sorry, I was preoccupied. Miles away."

"I've been looking for you. The other counselor I was telling you about? He's agreed to see you. I've made you an appointment for tomorrow morning, just after breakfast."

"Yes. Thank you. No. Wait! I'm supposed to be seeing Brother Macon then."

"I've already cleared it with him. He thinks it's a grand idea, by the way. Says he should have thought of it himself."

"So does this mean I won't have any more sessions with—"

"Not at all. He just rescheduled you to the evening. After supper. Is that all right?"

"Sure. I guess. No, it's fine. Sorry. I'm still a bit preoccupied."

"No problem. I caught you by surprise."

She trudged off down the walk, and I continued to my room.

My head had cleared by the time I got there, so I had no trouble noticing that my door was no longer latched.

I stepped inside, took a quick look around to make sure there was no one else there, then took my time checking whether anything had been disturbed.

If the Abbot had come looking for me and I hadn't answered when she knocked, it wasn't unreasonable to think that she might have stuck her head in the door and called out to make sure.

On the other hand . . .

I continued my search, and my efforts were rewarded. The latch on my suitcase was open. I looked inside, and someone had clearly rummaged through its contents.

I breathed a sigh of relief that I had left my second Bible—the one I wasn't supposed to own—hidden safely in my office back at the parsonage. I had seriously considered bringing it with me, but changed my mind at the last moment. Now I was glad that I had.

So someone—probably the Abbot—had searched my room.

The question was why?

If it was the Abbot, then the answer was probably that she had grown more suspicious of my mission, and—I had to admit —rightfully so.

I had handled my earlier session with her badly. I knew that—had known it at the time, if I was honest. I would have been suspicious in her shoes.

The truth was, I wasn't cut out for this kind of mission. It was completely out of character for me. That should have been obvious to anyone—even to Brine. Maybe especially to Brine.

So why had he sent me?

Chapter 13

"Kinde's second counselor on that visit may have been the more significant one."

Silas Redford, *The Real Adam Kinde: An Experiment in Biography*

"THE GOOD NEWS is that after today no one will have to escort you to these sessions."

The Abbot had met me right after breakfast, and led me out of the common room toward the pond.

"Once I've introduced you, you'll be able to come and go yourself."

I already suspected where we were headed, and I was filled with equal parts anticipation and dread.

"Am I about to visit the Abbey's hermit?"

"He's just a man. His circumstances are a little different, but otherwise . . ."

We hiked in silence until we came to the fork in the trail.

"FEAR NOT! Please respect—"

The Abbot thrust her palm in front of the angel's face, silencing it.

"Do you recognize my access?"

The angel took a moment to respond.

"Yours. Not his."

"From this moment on, he has the same access I do."

The angel didn't reply.

"Do you understand what I just said?"

"I do."

"And will you comply?"

An even longer pause.

"I will."

We headed down the trail toward the hermitage.

"That," the Abbot muttered, "is the single most difficult angel I have ever had the pleasure of dealing with."

"Could you get it reassigned?"

"I've tried. The red tape is enormous. I suspect someone has their reasons for wanting this particular one. Can't imagine why."

We reached the hermitage and stepped up onto the little porch. The Abbot rapped sharply on the door.

"Come in!"

The Abbot opened the door, and stood back for me to pass. I entered ahead of her, but she didn't follow. She closed the door behind me, leaving me alone with the hermit.

The hermitage consisted of a single room which was organized in sharp contrast to Macon's workroom. The floor was swept. The few belongings were carefully arranged on two shelves. The altar was heating a green enameled teakettle. A bright orange teapot stood waiting on the counter beside it. The bed was made. A small bare wood table by the window held a game of Shadow for one, neatly laid out on its surface.

The hermit was sitting at one of the two chairs on either side of the table—the one facing the door. He looked up from his game and smiled.

There was something familiar about his smile, but I couldn't place it.

He gestured toward the other chair, and I sat facing him.

He scooped up the Shadow deck and fanned the cards out on the table, face up, without saying a word. Then he picked out some cards, and laid them out between us.

I didn't know what game he was playing, if it was a game. I half suspected that everyone in the Abbey must be an amateur conjurer.

He raised his eyebrows and waited in silence.

I stared at the cards.

And then I understood.

WE R BEING WATCHED

I nodded.

He picked up the cards and laid out some more.

DNT MNTION OSSEUS

And then I recognized that smile.

I GREW up on the Franklyn Estate, the only child of the estate manager and the inseparable friend of the heir, Boyd Franklyn.

Boyd's father was not an unusually pious man, but he was

very traditional. So, even though the custom was long out of fashion among holders, he supported a private chaplain on his estate.

Pastor Dean's duties in that office were minimal. My father's job was demanding by contrast. The result was that though my father was very present in my life, Pastor Dean was *always* present and always available to me.

By the time I was ten or eleven I had become very religious under his influence, and when he resigned his position at the estate, to become the chaplain of a seminary, I surprised my parents by asking to attend the same institution.

I was very happy there, and my friendship with Pastor Dean continued until I was seventeen.

That was when it happened.

I overheard Pastor Dean and Dr. Thomas—the head of the school—talking about "Osseus". I asked him about it, and he warned me not to repeat it or have anything to do with it. Later I found out that two professors from the seminary proper seemed to be somehow connected to the name.

One of those professors was Presbyter Brine.

Not long after that Pastor Dean left the seminary for another position, and I hadn't heard from him since.

I went on to seminary proper, was ordained, and graduated. When I became pastor of the church back in the village owned by the Franklyn estate, it turned out that Presbyter Brine had also left the seminary and was my immediate superior.

Then, a few months before Brine sent me to the Abbey, I had overheard him use the word once more. It had been in passing, about another matter entirely, and added nothing to the little I already knew—except that Brine was definitely still involved in a scheme with Osseus, and that the scheme was both illegal and immoral.

I stared at the cards.

DNT MNTION OSSEUS

The smile I had not recognized at first, buried under that enormous beard, belonged to Pastor Dean.

I looked up, and nodded—unsure of my ground.

He swept the cards up again, and laid some more out.

EVRYTHNG ELS OK

Then he smiled and said, "Have you forgotten our old game, Adam? Or don't you recognize me under all this hair?"

"Pastor Dean? Really? I didn't expect . . . I mean, I didn't know—"

"—that I had become a hermit? No reason that you should. It wasn't entirely my choice."

"Then you've been—"

"Accused of heresy, and found guilty."

"But what . . . what *kind* of heresy? I mean, I can't imagine . . ."

"I'm not allowed to talk about it. And that's not what you're here for, anyway."

"But this is awful."

"Not really. It's a much quieter life than I would choose for myself. But it's not a bad one. Mostly, I miss the opportunity to be useful to others—but then here *you* are."

"Well, it is good to see you again."

"And you."

He looked me over.

"You know, you're the spitting image of your father when I first knew him."

The teakettle whistled, and he got up to pour the water into the teapot. He reached a trivet down from the shelf, placed it on the table between us, and set the teapot on top of it. Then he placed a cup in front of each of us.

"So, Adam. You're here for counseling?"

"I am."

"Tell me."

I took a deep breath.

"You remember when you first taught me to pray?"

"I do."

"And how you told me that real prayer wasn't asking for things, or weaving some kind of spell with fancy words, but just being myself, in the presence of God?"

"I see your training was not in vain."

"Well that's the way it was for me. A sort of conversation—even though I was the only one talking. It was that way for years. I could sense God listening silently to everything I said, and it made a real difference."

"I'm glad."

"Except, one day not long ago, I tried to pray, and God was gone. And it's been that way ever since."

"And that's why you're here."

"That's why."

"You've been talking to Brother Macon about this, as well?"

I nodded.

"And what has he told you?"

"He's been teaching me theology. Stuff I never heard before. But I can't see the relevance."

"What kind of stuff?"

"Oh, about the Holy Duality, about the image of God in humans—that and a bunch of magic tricks."

He chuckled.

"I see. Well, you may not be any happier with me, at first. I'd like to give you a song from scripture to contemplate."

He gave me the reference, and I looked it up in my Bible:

Blessed is one whose faith is in God.

    Who is like a tree planted by the stream.

    Its leaves remain green when the heat comes.

    It bears fruit in the year of drought.

He poured the tea as I read the passage out loud. The hot steam smelled of cloves and oranges.

"Well," he said, "what do you make of that passage?"

"Can I be honest?"

"We won't get very far if you aren't."

"It's different from what Brother Macon gave me, but . . ."

"But?"

"The problem with his approach is that I can't see any connection to my problem. With this I can see a connection, but—to be honest—it's no help."

"Why not?"

"All it says is 'have faith in God, and everything will be fine.' That may be true, but it doesn't address my difficulty."

"Thank you for being honest. It saves time for both of us. Will you carry out an assignment for me?"

"Of course."

"Then I'll tell you that you're completely wrong about that passage. You couldn't be more wrong. And the assignment is to contemplate it until you see why."

"Everyone's giving me puzzles to contemplate."

"Really?"

"Well, not everyone. Just you and Presbyter Brine."

He sat up a little straighter.

"You talk to Brine?"

"He's my superior. He sent me here on this fact-finding mission."

He gave that some thought before responding—cautiously, I thought.

"This puzzle he gave you. What was it, exactly?"

I realized my mistake. But this was Pastor Dean, and he was not one of Brine's suspects.

"He told me about a heresy he once avoided. He had come down on the right side of it, but he said he had done that for the wrong reason. Then he asked me to consider why his reason was the wrong one."

"I see."

I waited for him to say more, but he didn't. I sipped my tea. It was sweet, and spicy. After a very long silence, I wondered if he even remembered I was there.

Finally, I gave up.

"Well," I said, "I should probably go."

He granted me a sort of absent glance.

"Yes," he said, "Of course. I'll see you next time."

I let myself out, and hiked back toward my room.

I wasn't sure I should have told him about Brine. Brine had advised me to stay clear of him, but that wasn't the only reason. It was also because I had seen something while I was there. Something that made me wonder whether he wasn't more involved than I thought.

His belt was a chain. Exactly like Brother Macon's.

Chapter 14

"A certain pastor wanted a bigger church building. He wished to have God's blessing on this plan, so he 'laid out a fleece'—asking God to give him a sign. The sign he requested was the church board's approval of the project. He then proceeded to do everything he could to influence that vote."

Ram Jacobs, Senior Fellow, Mens Dei, *Prolegomena to an Integrated Worldview*

AFTER SUPPER BROTHER EARNEST took me back to the research facility. We passed a group of monks clearing an area in front of the entrance. They were in good spirits, joking among themselves, and waved merrily at us as we passed.

Earnest grinned at me.

"They're preparing the ground for Stonesday. I'm afraid

there's an informal, but long-standing, tradition at the Abbey of excessive drinking on Stoneseve."

"Am I keeping you from honoring the tradition?"

He shook his head.

"No. On two counts, actually."

"Two?"

"First, I'm not allowed to indulge as much as others, because of my position. But second because I'll be dropping you off in a couple of minutes, and then I'll be free to join them."

The path was unlit at night, and so we journeyed on through the darkness, a starry sky overhead.

When we got to the facility, Brother Earnest opened the door and led me through the entry hall and around the corner toward the lair of the Master Wright.

We could hear someone singing as we approached.

Earnest laughed.

"Sounds like you'll be joining the festivities as well."

When we got to the door it was clear that he was right. Brother Macon's voice was raised in song on the other side.

Earnest opened the door and patted me on the back before leaving.

"Good luck!"

My spiritual counselor stood in the middle of the room, a coffee cup in one hand and a bottle in the other, his voice raised in a Resurrection carol.

His eyes met mine, but he didn't miss a note. The only indication that he had seen me enter was a subtle shift in his manner. He was now singing the carol to *me*.

I stayed where I was, waiting, my eyes on his, until he had finished—which he did with a flourish.

"Ah! My disciple has arrived! Allow me, dear disciple,

to . . . to *initiate* you . . . initiate you into the mysteries of Stone-seve at Saint Isaac's Abbey! An old and venerated custom!"

He waved the bottle, beckoning me to enter, then gave his full attention to a careful survey of the room.

"There is, I am sure, somewhere here . . . somewhere . . . Ha!"

He spied one of the numerous coffee cups which littered the work-tables and pounced on it.

"A chalice, a grail, a *holy* grail for our guest . . . for my disciple. Did you come seeking the holy grail, disciple?"

He tipped the bottle into the cup, and dispensed an extravagant amount of its contents. Then he pressed the cup into my hands.

"Drink up, my friend. It's holy water."

I hesitated, quite sure that the cup had not been cleaned recently.

If ever.

He picked his own cup back up, and urged me again.

"Don't be shy, man. Drink!"

I took a tentative sip. It was quite good.

He clapped me on the back, raised the bottle, and sloshed a bit more into my cup.

"So what brings you, disciple, on this eve to my . . . my . . . Oh! You're here for my counsel, to help you deal with the absence, the absence of the presence, the presence of the absence . . . the *appearance* of . . ."

And with that he sat down, suddenly and hard, on the floor.

He waved his cup toward a chair.

"Have a seat, my friend, and we shall discuss the secrets of creation."

I sat, and he sat up straighter and cross-legged in front of me.

"The master sits at the feet of the disciple. This demonstrates his humility. How can I serve you?"

I pulled Lilith's gift from my pocket.

"Let me give you this, before I forget. It's from Sister Edith."

"Ah! The lady reciprocates. Excellent. Could you put it on the table there? But I am serious. Ask me anything, and I will supply you with answers. Not necessarily the *correct* answers, mind you. But the best I have at my disposal."

I saw an opportunity.

"Are you a heretic?"

He straightened a bit, and suddenly appeared slightly more sober.

"Is that why you're really here? To persecute heretics?"

"It's just that some of the things you've told me . . ."

He nodded sagely.

"I see. Do I get to ask you questions as well?"

"I suppose."

"Are you an agent of the big 'O'?"

I mustered my most innocent expression.

"The big 'O'?"

He leaned forward, searching my face.

"You, my disciple, overestimate your skill at dissimulation. You understand me. So answer the question."

I had to think about it. I realized it was a question I had carefully managed not to ask myself.

"No," I said finally, "at least not *intentionally*."

"Not intentionally. Well said. You may be more worthy than I realized."

"Worthy of what?"

"The holy grail. But I must answer *your* question. My short answer is 'No.'" That is, of course, the answer any heretic would also give."

"And the longer answer?"

"A longer answer would be 'Yes. Isn't everyone?'"

He hiccuped.

"But I'm afraid you would find that unsatisfying as well."

"Do you have a satisfying answer?"

He became pensive.

"The *satisfying* answer depends on you."

"Whether *you* are a heretic depends on *me*?"

He leaned forward and seemed to be having trouble focusing.

"What is *your* source of truth?"

"The scriptures, obviously."

He downed the remaining contents of his mug, refilled it, and took another gulp. Then he swayed to one side, caught himself, and managed to sit up straight again.

"The scriptures. Quite right. Now as to your question about the genealogy of Joshua . . ."

I was losing him.

"That wasn't the question I asked."

"Oh. No. Not the . . . Not the right . . . When God created Adam, he formed him from clay, you see . . . then he breathed . . . God breathed . . ."

And he slowly tipped sideways, until his shoulder hit the ground. The contents of his cup spilled across the floor.

I took the bottle from his other hand and set it up on the table next to Lilith's gift, then I found a towel near his altar and used that to wipe the floor.

I wouldn't have been able to lift him if I'd tried, so I just pulled a blanket off his bed and put it over him.

He was snoring loudly as I closed the door behind me.

My last words to Lucky had not gone well.

I had been standing in our living room at the parsonage, peering out the front window, waiting for Presbyter Brine's chariot to arrive. It was a warm morning and the sun streamed in through the window, throwing bright squares onto the wooden floor.

We had eaten breakfast in silence—bacon and eggs and Lucky's amazing pancakes. He had brought out his homemade marmalade to sweeten them. I didn't know whether he was still trying to soften me up, or if he was just making our last breakfast together memorable.

His silence had given me no clue.

And standing in the living room, gazing out the window, I was secretly hoping that it would continue, that Lucky wouldn't come out of the kitchen before I left, so that I could leave with our silence intact.

But he did, of course—folding his apron as he crossed the room.

"Well, lad, I hope you have a successful trip."

"Yes. I do too."

"About that matter we discussed a week ago . . ."

"I'd rather forget the whole thing. Put it behind us."

"I can't, lad. This is something I have to do, and I won't lie to you about it. Not to you."

"I don't know what to say, Lucky."

He was motionless for a moment, then breathed again.

"Should I bother to come back, then?"

I didn't have an answer to that—not one I had words for. But I was rescued—temporarily at least—by the arrival of Brine's chariot.

"I have to go."

I grabbed my stick and suitcase and headed for the door.

As the chariot left the ground, Lucky waved to me from the front steps.

I pretended not to see.

I DIDN'T SLEEP WELL after my session with Brother Macon. I kept thinking about Lucky, about the Abbot and Pastor Dean and Lilith. About people I liked or loved or had loved, and how I seemed to be on the verge of betraying them all.

So I tossed and I turned throughout the night, waking time again to uncomfortable thoughts and wishing I had drunk more of Brother Macon's brew.

Just before dawn it became obvious that I wasn't going to sleep again, so I dressed and made my bed and wandered down to the common room.

There was hot water on a small altar in the corner and teabags on a shelf. The fire was already blazing in the fireplace. I sank into the couch in front of the flames.

The problem was that I had responsibilities as well as friendships. I had a duty of obedience to Presbyter Brine, and to the church as well. And to God. To the throne at the top of the chain of being.

There were times I wished I had never gone to seminary, never been ordained, never taken on those duties.

I had wanted, so much, to *know*. To plumb the secrets of God and meaning and the whole world of my religion. I had thought that seminary would give me that knowledge. But the last few days had taught me that it apparently didn't even do that.

Not that those few days had been a success in any other way. I hadn't uncovered any proof of heresy—didn't even really have a clear idea of what heresy I was looking for.

And I certainly hadn't made any progress on my private spiritual problem. All I got from my counselors were riddles of one sort or another. I was beginning to doubt if they were the kind of counselors I needed.

"Hi!"

I looked up into Lilith's smiling face.

"Mind if I join you?"

I moved over, and she sat beside me, holding her own teacup and staring into the fire.

"Did you give Brother Macon my gift?"

"Last night."

"What did he say?"

"He didn't open it. Actually, I'm not sure he knew I gave it to him. He was pretty intoxicated at the time."

Neither of us spoke for a long time.

It was good to sit beside her again. Comfortable.

That might have been what gave me the idea.

"Lilith?"

"Mm-hm?"

"Joshuans are a mystical order, right?"

"Mm-hm."

"Do you do spiritual counseling?"

"Joshuans in general, or me in particular?"

"I meant you in particular."

"Heavens, no! I'd be rubbish at it."

"Oh."

"Why?"

"Nothing important. I just have this little spiritual difficulty, and the Abbot has set me up with a counselor—well, two counselors, actually—but they don't seem to be helping, so . . ."

"So you thought I might help."

"Yeah."

"It can't be that little, if the Abbot thinks you need two counselors."

"Well, the first one wasn't helping, so I guess she just thought . . ."

"I get it. Does this problem have to do with that girl you haven't gotten over?"

"It's a problem with prayer."

"I wouldn't know anything about that."

"But you're a Joshuan."

"Well, *doing* and *teaching* are two quite different things. Have you talked to your superior about this problem?"

"Presbyter Brine? Hardly."

"Presbyter Brine is your boss?"

"Well, supervisor. Yeah, I guess, in a sense."

"Is he as strange as they say?"

"He's pretty strange."

"Some people think he's positively evil. Do you trust him?"

"Brine? I don't know that trust comes into it. I owe him obedience."

Chapter 15

"Had that pastor honestly sought a sign, he might have asked God to keep all of the cars in the parking lot from starting for two hours exactly after a given church service. But this he did not do for two reasons: he did not expect a real sign was possible, and he would not risk a sign that went against his wish."

Ram Jacobs, Senior Fellow, Mens Dei, *Prolegomena to an Integrated Worldview*

LILITH and I had run out of things to say, and had resumed our silence, side by side, watching the flames. We must have been there an hour when the Abbot found us.

"Enjoying the fire—or the quiet?"

I looked up.

"Both, actually."

"Well, I won't disturb you. I just wanted to tell you that your schedule has changed for the day. You and Macon apparently had quite a party last night. He's taking the day off to recover for this evening's ceremony."

"I hope he's not suffering too much."

"Given the cause, I'd say he's suffering just enough. You seem fine. No hangover?"

"He started without me. And he finished after I had only been there a short time. I should probably be grateful."

"Well, I've brought that other example—the one that's better than the duck/rabbit picture—if you're interested. We could meet after lunch, since you won't be visiting Macon."

"You sure you want to work on Stonesday?"

"I'm sure I *don't*. Which is why I'm suggesting this instead."

Breakfast was minimal—dry cereal with milk—as befitted Stonesday.

After spending so much time in Brother Macon's workroom, I was doubly impressed by the sense of light and order in the Abbot's office. I did prefer the aroma of coffee to the smell of cleaning fluid, but you can't have everything.

She motioned me to take a seat, then pulled out a green rectangular block, just slightly larger than a deck of Shadow cards, and exactly the same shape. She moved her stylus around the back of it for a few moments, then placed it on the table in front of me and tapped the surface once with her finger.

"Look at the block, and tell me what you see."

I stared at the block, it was just a block—probably of monkstone, but I couldn't even be sure of that.

I was about to say so, when suddenly an image flashed briefly on the surface. It was gone before I could think about it, but I knew exactly what it was.

"A *P* of spades."

"Very good. Any doubt at all?"

"None."

She tapped the surface once more.

"Try again."

Once again I waited, and after a moment another card appeared and vanished.

I spoke without hesitation.

"An *S* of diamonds."

She tapped again.

"An *F*," I said, "of hearts."

And again.

"*B* of clubs."

"Any doubts? About any of those?"

"No. Should I have?"

"You were viewing those at three hundredths of a second, yet you had no trouble identifying them at all. Now let's try thirty-three hundreths—a full third of a second."

She applied her stylus to the back of the block again, then set it in front of me and gave it a tap.

This time they didn't seem as clear.

"It's a *P*, I think, but I can't make out the suit."

Tap.

"*S*, but it . . . it doesn't even look like a card!"

Tap.

"I'm not sure of the suit. I . . . I seem to have forgotten what a heart looks like."

Tap.

"This is absurd! I can't even tell what color it is! What is this thing doing?"

The Abbot pulled the block back.

"Take a deep breath, and let it out slowly."

My breath was ragged. It took me a moment to calm down.

She smiled.

"Better?"

I nodded.

"What was I looking at?"

"The same images you viewed the first time. You just got to see them for about ten times as long."

"But what were they? They weren't cards."

"Shall I let you see them for a little longer? Let's give you a full second this time."

She made another adjustment and placed the block before me.

Tap.

"Of course. What was I thinking? It's a *P* of spades, but it's red instead of black!"

Tap.

"A black S of diamonds!"

She pulled the block back, made another adjustment.

"Let's try the last two at the original speed—three hundredths of a second."

Tap.

"A black *F* of hearts."

Tap.

"A red *B* of clubs."

"Very good. Now let's talk about what just happened, and what it means."

"Please."

"When you came into my office, you had already created a set of categories about Shadow cards—probably when you were a child. A set of possible letters, and a set of possible suits. Yes?"

"Four suits," I said. "Spades, diamonds, hearts, and clubs."

"And, to quote Brother Macon, in 'your world' diamonds and hearts were red, and spades and clubs were black."

"Right."

She pushed the duck/rabbit picture across the table.

"Remember this? Remember how the way you looked at it made it appear to be either a duck or a rabbit?"

"And?"

"So suppose, for a moment, that a creature existed which fit this drawing far better than either a duck or a rabbit—a creature you had never seen or heard of. Could you see that creature by looking at this drawing?"

"No. I wouldn't know what to look for."

"Or, to put it another way, you wouldn't have created a category for that creature, and so you wouldn't be able to see it."

She let that sink in, then continued.

"We tend to think that we first *see* something, and then *categorize* it. That we see a duck, or a teacup, or a stylus, and only then decide what it is. But that's not true. We don't perceive things first and *then* categorize them. We see them *by categorizing* them."

"I think I understand."

"The only way for you to see a red spade would be for you to either have the category of 'red spades' in your world already, or, when faced with an anomaly, to create that category. This is what happens when we encounter mystery."

"Mystery?"

"The gap between our creation and God's. That's what an anomaly is."

"So why didn't I have trouble the first time you showed me the cards?"

"I gave you so little time that you were able to ignore the anomaly. So you just saw something that fit your already created categories."

"And the second time, you gave me just enough time to . . ."

"To encounter the mystery. To experience the anomaly."

"To sense the difference between my creation and God's."

"Exactly."

"But wasn't it really *your* creation?"

"God created me, so all of my creation is a part of God's creation, just as yours is. Perhaps it would be better just to use the word 'reality.'"

"Whatever you call it, it was unsettling."

"Encounters with mystery often are."

"And then, when you gave me even more time, I was able to create new categories."

"And once you had done that, you could see the anomalous cards just as easily as the traditional ones."

"Because I already had a category for them."

"Yes."

"And I suppose this has something to do with my 'fleecer lessons'?"

"And life in general. We're all going through this process—encountering mystery—all the time, only it usually happens so fast that we don't notice it. You only needed to view an anomalous card for a one full second to form your new category, to make it part of your own creation. But you weren't aware of 'forming a new category' at all, so you never experienced a gap between your categories and reality."

"Right. It just felt like I was seeing it more clearly."

"But when I only gave you a third of a second, you didn't have time to form a new category, but you *did* have time enough to notice that your old ones didn't fit."

"So I experienced the encounter with mystery—with the difference between my world and God's."

"Exactly."

"And fleecers?"

"We learn about God by encountering the mystery of his creation, but because we are trying to understand at deeper levels we have to be more conscious of the process. Whether we're studying light or human nature, we have to be very aware of our dependence on anomalies—on things that don't fit the world we're creating. If we don't notice them, we can't bring our creations closer to God's."

"And that's what fleeces are for?"

"I THINK I'm beginning to see what they're getting at."

Pastor Dean looked up from the tea he was pouring. We were sitting on either side of the same table in the hermitage, the afternoon light gleaming on the snow outside the window.

"And what," he asked, "are they getting at?"

I struggled to put my thoughts together in some coherent fashion.

"Well, everything the Abbot is teaching me about fleecing, and all the magic tricks and talk of humans as creators that I'm getting from Brother Macon, all add up to the same thing."

He set a teacup in front of me and waited for me to finish.

"It's all about connecting with God, but through his creation, you see? And my problem, when you get down to it, is a lack of connecting with God."

He took a sip of his tea, watching me over the rim, then set it carefully in front of him.

"And you find this enlightening?"

"Maybe. A little."

"Is it helpful—does it help resolve your problem?"

I laughed.

"Not at all."

"Hmm. So how many ways—before your problem, that is—how many ways did you have of connecting with God?"

"Two, I guess. The scriptures and prayer."

"And you're saying that Brother Macon and the Abbot have shown you a third way?"

I took a sip of tea, and the spicy sweetness filled my head.

"I guess so—like the way you would connect with an artist, through his paintings—or a musician through his music."

"But that approach doesn't work as well for you as prayer did."

"Exactly."

"Why not?"

I considered that.

"I think it's because it's not *personal* enough, if that makes sense."

"It makes sense to me. Why do you think that is?"

"It's all so . . . so second-hand I guess. Even if I make my creation very close to God's creation, it's still *my* creation I'm living in. I'm not experiencing God, or even God's creation, but my own set of categories."

"And you need something more immediate?"

"Yes. Like prayer used to be."

"But was it? Really?"

"What do you mean?"

"Tell me, when you prayed before, where was God?"

"God is everywhere."

"Yes. But when you prayed, where did you *experience* God to be?"

"What?"

"You were talking to God, right? And the presence was real to you? Where? In front of you or behind you?"

"Oh. You're right. In front of me."

"And on a level with you, or below, or—"

"Slightly above me."

"Why do you think that was?"

"I don't know. I guess that's just where I imagined . . . Oh."

"So you want something more immediate than even that?"

"I don't know. I guess that may not be possible."

"I didn't say that. I'll give you a second thing to contemplate, along with the song I gave you before. *What part of God's creation can you experience without your own categories?*"

"I have no idea."

"Think about it."

Chapter 16

"Whatever the personal implications of his visit to the Abbey, there is no question that the events there had a significant effect on his advancement within the Church hierarchy."

Silas Redford, *The Real Adam Kinde: An Experiment in Biography*

I HADN'T BROUGHT my Bible to my visits with Pastor Dean after the first time. There was no good reason for it, even though I knew something that he might or might not have known.

When he told me through the Shadow cards that we were being watched, he meant, of course, by his guardian angel. What he might not have known was that the angel needed a Bible, or some other monkstone object, in order to be present.

Since Pastor Dean's Bible was always right there, in plain site, it didn't really matter if I brought mine or not. But I had this sort of superstitious need not to help an angel eavesdrop on our conversations—especially *that* angel.

So I didn't receive the two words that had been left on my Bible until I got back to my room.

The first was from the Abbot, asking me to come to her office as soon as I got the message.

The second was from Presbyter Brine, apologizing for . . . ahhh . . . inconveniencing me, and saying that it really couldn't be helped, and craving . . . craving my cooperation.

When I got to the Abbot's office, she was busy on her own Bible, but waved me to a seat while she finished.

When she had, she looked up and let out an enormous sigh.

"Have you heard from Presbyter Brine?"

"I got a very unenlightening message from him, begging my cooperation in some unmentioned matter."

She nodded and scowled.

"Coward."

She had a bottle and two shot glasses waiting on her desk. She poured both glasses full, and pushed one toward me. I shook my head, and pushed it back.

"Well," she said, "I guess it's down to me then."

She drained her glass, then looked me in the eyes.

"Brother Macon is dead."

"*Dead?* I didn't think . . . When I left him he was drunk enough, but he seemed—"

"Take a breath, Pastor. I talked to him this morning, remember? And he was fine then. A little hungover, but fine otherwise."

"Right. Of course. So how?"

"There's no pleasant way to put this. He appears to have been murdered."

"Murdered? But why? Who would . . . are you sure?"

"I found him lying on the floor of his workroom this afternoon with a knife in his abdomen. So yes, reasonably sure."

"Brother Macon. That's so . . . I'm so sorry. You were close to him, I know."

I pushed my chair back.

"I suppose Brine is cutting my mission short, then. Would it be okay with you if I stayed for the service? I would like to pay my—"

"You're not going anywhere. I requested an ecclesiastical judge to deal with this matter. It happened on Abbey soil and the victim is a monk, so it's entirely in the church's hands."

"So Presbyter Brine wants me to assist him?"

"He can't come."

"Then assist whoever—"

"He's deputized you."

"Deputized?"

"You are the ecclesiastical judge appointed to investigate."

I pulled my shot glass back toward me.

As we walked to the research building, I struggled to find an ecclesiastical judge persona in me somewhere. I had not felt competent for my original mission, but this was beyond reason.

Brother Earnest was standing guard at the door to the workroom when we arrived.

"I left Earnest here," the Abbot said, "just to make sure. We're the only two besides Macon to have access to this room, so it's secure even without a guard, but still . . ."

She opened the door on what at first glance was an empty workroom—just as cluttered as always, but apparently unoccupied. The aroma of coffee was accompanied by the faintly metallic smell of blood.

We had to walk around the firmament to see his body on the floor.

He lay on his right side, his right hand clutching the handle of a knife. Its blade was buried in his abdomen. His left arm half covered his face, as though he had been reaching for the leg of the worktable behind him when he died.

I turned to the Abbot.

"Did you . . . has anyone touched him, or moved anything?"

"I felt for a pulse when I found him. Then I sent word for a healer, who confirmed that he was dead. But I wouldn't let them move him, since it was obvious there would be an investigation."

"And the room's been locked since then? No one else came in?"

"I summoned Earnest, and posted him at the door with instructions to make sure."

"When did you find him?"

"Macon? After lunch, about the time you were on your way to the hermit. I came down to see how his hangover was faring, walked in as usual, and found him here, just like this."

"Do you see anything other than the body that's unusual for this room, or out of place?"

She glanced around the room.

"Nothing at first glance, anyway."

"Okay."

I gathered my thoughts.

"I think the best approach would be for you to stand over by the door, if you don't mind, being careful not to touch anything, while I have a look around. That way I can ask you about anything that puzzles me."

The truth was I didn't want to be in that room at all. And I really didn't want to be there alone.

She moved to the door, and I stood over the body, forcing myself to think about what must have happened. I found myself thinking out loud, to break the awful silence.

"The knife goes straight in, at a right angle to the body. And it goes in deep. So whoever did it had to be strong . . ."

I pantomimed a horizontal knife thrust.

". . . and they had to be fairly tall, or the knife would have gone in at an angle."

I looked up at the Abbot.

"Tell me if any of this sounds wrong to you. I'm making it up as I go along."

She nodded. I continued.

"He apparently tried to drag himself toward the work table, probably to help him stand."

His toes were about a foot away from the stand we had found him behind on the day I first met him.

"He may have been standing in position to use the firmament."

The firmament was empty and silent. So he hadn't turned it on yet. And there were no disks in the tray.

"But if he was standing there, behind the tray, then the . . . I might as well get used to the word . . . the *killer* couldn't have been standing in front of him. I suppose they could have reached around from behind, but it seems unlikely—the knife goes straight in. Maybe he was just *near* the tray, and facing his killer."

I glanced at the Abbot again.

"Any ideas? Am I missing anything so far?"

"I really hate to say it, but yes, you are."

"What?"

"The knife could have been *thrown*, from where I'm standing now. It is a throwing knife."

She was right. I'd missed that. But it still didn't make sense.

"Lilith doesn't have access to this room."

"But *I* do. And someone could have let *her* in. Also—just because we only know of two good throwers at the Abbey doesn't make us the only two."

"By someone else letting her in, you mean Earnest?"

"Either Earnest or Macon himself, since I know I didn't. But you'd have to consider me for that as well."

"You think I should treat you as a suspect?"

"I think you pretty much have to. I certainly didn't do it in *my* creation, but you're stuck working from yours."

Something else caught my eye. There was a disk on the floor, not far from one of the worktables. I went over to pick it up.

It was just a blank, but when I bent over I could see something else under the table—Lilith's gift box. It had been opened. I fished it out and examined it.

"What's that?" said the Abbot.

"It's a gift box. A gift from Lilith—from Sister Edith. I delivered it to him last night."

"What's in it?"

"Nothing. Apparently he opened it. Why do you ask?"

She shrugged.

"I don't know, really."

I had no idea what to do next, so I tried to sound competent.

"I'll probably have to come back again. Can you keep this room untouched for now?"

"You want me to leave his body here?"

I hadn't thought of that, either.

"No. Of course not. But make sure the healers don't touch anything else when they take it."

"And you might want to move that coffeepot off of the altar."

"Yes. Good idea."

I moved the pot.

"Anything else you can think of?"

"I think you're doing fine."

I took the opportunity to question Brother Earnest as we were leaving.

No, he hadn't let anyone else into Brother Macon's workroom that day. He hadn't let anyone in since me, the previous evening.

No, he hadn't come to the workroom himself during that period.

Yes, he totally understood why I had to ask. He had spent the morning and early afternoon with other monks, preparing for the evening ceremony, and yes, he could give me their names.

No, no one had tried to enter while he was guarding the door that afternoon.

I told him I would get those names later if I needed them, and the Abbot and I left him there, guarding the door.

Chapter 17

"We stand at a turning point. Our system is designed to feed the wealth produced by the creativity and labor of the common mob into the coffers of the well-bred, and it has succeeded beyond our dreams. But we did not anticipate the effects of that success."

Oss Taylor, founder of Mens Dei. Initial Address to the First Committee.

I WANTED some time to think—to sort out how to tackle this puzzle.

And I wanted to try to sort out the spiritual difficulties it brought me as well.

It was not lost on me that I faced exactly the kind of temptation the Abbot's fleecers faced. I didn't have a pet theory—not yet, anyway—but I did have some conclusions I wanted very much to avoid.

When I got to my room, I realized I was still holding the blank disk I had picked up from Brother Macon's floor. I started to put it into my pocket, then stopped myself abruptly.

I already had the disk he had given me from his magic trick in that pocket, and I didn't want to get the two mixed up. It wasn't all that rational, since they were identical—but now the disk he had given me was not just a spiritual exercise. It was a sort of reminder of him, and everything he had done for me.

At that moment I realized I was personally involved. He had, in the process of few short sessions, become more than a counselor. He had become a friend.

I dropped the disk in my hand onto the top of the dresser, and sat on the edge of the bed. The tears backed up behind my eyes.

How had that happened, in so short a time? I was not just the visiting judge; I was one of the mourners as well. And the same thing had happened with the Abbot. She was a friend too. That was why this whole thing was going to be so difficult. And, of course, Lilith. I even suspected it would be hard for me to find Brother Earnest guilty.

Brother Macon was dead. He would never do another magic trick, never drink too much on Stoneseve again. He would never patiently lead me, or anyone, along one of his strange paths of thought.

Brine had dropped me into an intolerable situation, whether he knew it or not. Whether he cared or not.

But mine was not to reason why. I had a job to do, and I needed to figure out how to do it. I steeled myself for the task.

I opened my Bible, and started a list:

1) Are there any other throwers in the Abbey?
2) Where was Lilith when Brother Macon died?
3) Where was Brother Earnest?
4) Could someone else have had access?
5) Was anyone else around the facility?
6) Who would want him dead, and why?
7) Where did the knife come from?

I stopped there. It wasn't the most important point, but it was something I could check immediately, and it was physical. I was quite ready to leave my thoughts alone for a while and actually *do* something instead.

IT MIGHT HAVE BEEN WARMING a bit, or I might have just gotten used to the cold. Or perhaps I was too focused on the situation I'd found myself in to feel it.

The clearing was unchanged, except for the lack of footprints. Snow had fallen sometime since my previous visit with Lilith and the Abbot. I added that to my list:

8) Find out when last snowfall was.

It might be important to know the latest time that someone could have visited there.

I went straight to the shed and opened the door. There on the back wall hung the array of throwing knives.

And two were missing.

Two.

So the killer—I was getting used to that word—the killer had gotten their weapon from the shed.

And they had taken two knives.

Why two?

A backup?

Not if they were planning to stab Brother Macon by hand.

And if the knife had been thrown, it was thrown with such precision that it seemed unlikely they would have needed a backup.

Possibly a backup then, if it was thrown—but probably not.

Probably, the killer was planning two deaths.

So time was critical now. I needed to find the killer before they killed again.

I examined every inch of the shed in detail. I don't know what I thought I was looking for. A thread, perhaps, from a coat? A lost piece of jewelry?

A note, confessing to the crime?

I just didn't want to miss anything.

When I finished there, I gave the same treatment to the entire clearing, examining the target at the far end in detail, even the hedge at the entrance.

I came up with nothing, but felt a little better for the effort.

As I left, I remembered leaving with the Abbot the previous Tuesday. And I remembered Lilith, staying behind to put the knives away.

***

RETURNING FROM THE CLEARING, I stepped up on the porch and passed the Abbot's office and her tinkling chimes without any definite plan. The monks were still at work on Stonesday preparations. They had cleared the snow from a large circle of ground in front of the Abbey, and were piling stones, each about the size of a cantaloupe, at regular intervals around the circumference.

I watched them work for a moment or two, then stopped one of them, and asked him if he could take a moment to talk to me.

He wiped his hand across his forehead.

"Take all the time you like, Pastor. It just means I get a little break."

"So you know who I am?"

"And I know why you're asking questions. It's about Brother Macon, right?"

"I've been appointed as the ecclesiastical judge, so I have to try to sort out exactly what happened."

"You mean who killed him."

"Eventually. I'm just getting started at the moment. You and these others have been preparing this circle for the ceremony tonight?"

"Yes."

"And that means shoveling out all of the snow?"

"It does."

"So would you remember when the last time it snowed was?"

"I sure would. It snowed pretty heavily late Thursday night —just before we started. We were afraid it would snow again and undo all of yesterday's work, but it didn't."

"That's really helpful. One other thing. I'm starting out by trying to narrow the field. I want to eliminate as many people as possible. Is this the same group that was working on the circle last night?"

He let his eyes roam over his fellow monks.

"Except for Andrew over there. He was on duty in the kitchen last night. And Earnest joined us sometime after dark."

"And this same group has been at work here all day?"

"Starting after breakfast, and breaking for lunch, yes."

"Was anybody missing at lunch?"

That took him a moment.

"I don't think so. We all went in together, and all came right back here."

"Was Brother Earnest with you today?"

"Most of the time. He has other duties, so he comes and goes. I think he was here all morning, and right after lunch for a while, but then he was called off, and hasn't been back."

I thanked him and headed back to the Abbot's office.

She looked up as I opened the door.

"What do you need, Pastor?"

"Just a question. When was the last time you communicated with Brother Macon before you found his body?"

"When he sent word that he was taking the day off."

"Can you remember when that was?"

"Oh. I see. It was right after I got to my desk. Shortly after dawn. So it happened sometime between then and when I found him."

"And that target and knife cabinet in the clearing. Were they already here when you first came to the Abbey?"

"No. I had them put in when I was made Abbot, so I could practice. And you're right. That makes it less likely that there was already a thrower here."

"I was thinking the other way round—that if they *had* been here already it would imply that there *was* another thrower. I don't think it actually rules anything out. You've never seen anyone else use the target?"

"I haven't."

"Well, there's that."

Chapter 18

"In a hundred years, we will no longer need the mob for labor, and they will no longer have the income to act as consumers. Division between races and division between science and religion will then only make them less docile, and more difficult to control. The time has come to change tactics."

Oss Taylor, founder of Mens Dei. Address to the First Committee.

LILITH ANSWERED her door wearing the same dark green cloak she had worn on the day we arrived. She fell into my arms, sobbing on my shoulder.

I held her there for a while, then backed her slowly into her room so I could reach behind me with one hand and close the door against the cold.

After a time she straightened, then looked up at me with a desperate face. I gave her a final hug, and she moved to sit on the edge of her bed, next to her suitcase.

I put myself in the chair and waited for her to speak.

It took her some time.

Finally she looked up, offered me an apologetic smile, and said, "We were very close."

"You and Brother Macon."

She nodded.

"We were *too* close, given his vows. I wouldn't have cared, but he—he did. That was the real reason I took my meals in my room. It wasn't part of my retreat. It was for us—for him—to avoid temptation."

"You had agreed not to see each other in person."

"Yes."

"And that was why you exchanged gifts through me."

She nodded.

"I was supposed to leave today, this afternoon. But now . . ."

"Now you'll be staying for the funeral?"

She nodded again.

"Do they know," she asked, "does anyone know who . . ."

"Who killed him? Not yet. It seems it's up to me to find out."

"You?"

"I've been appointed ecclesiastical judge."

"Oh."

"So I should tell you that you may not be allowed to leave, even after the funeral, if I haven't figured out what happened by then."

"Do you have any idea? At all?"

"Not really. Do you have any idea who might have wanted to harm him?"

She shook her head, then had a thought.

"It probably doesn't mean anything, but . . ."

"What?"

"We did send a word to each other from time to time."

"And?"

"Well, he and the Abbot weren't quite as friendly as they appeared. That is, they *were* friends, but something had come between them."

"Really? Could I see those words?"

"I didn't keep them. Parts were a little . . ."

She blushed.

". . . a little embarrassing."

"Did he say what they disagreed about?"

"He was vague about that. I think the Abbot had done something, something Macon thought was wrong. He was torn about whether to confront her about it."

"Hmm."

"I'm sure it's nothing. The Abbot couldn't possibly have . . ."

It struck me that she didn't know the weapon was a throwing knife. If the Abbot and the healers had kept their mouths shut, perhaps no one did. And no one but me and the killer knew there were two knives missing.

I decided not to enlighten her just yet.

"It was right of you to tell me. Before I leave you to unpack again, I have to ask you some other questions. Sorry, but it has to be done."

"No. I understand."

"What did you do today between the time we were sitting by the fire and about an hour after lunch?"

"I came up to my room and waited for breakfast. Brother Andrew, I think, brought it. When I finished, I left the dishes for him outside the door and took a walk up toward the cemetery. There's a bench there, about a third of the way from the hermitage to the cemetery. I meditated on the bench until I heard the lunch bell, then went back to my room, in time for lunch. Another monk—one I don't know—brought my lunch, and I ate in my room."

"Did you see anyone else on your walk?"

"I don't think so. I'm pretty sure I didn't."

The bell for supper rang in the distance.

I stood.

"I'm sorry for—sorry about Macon."

I pulled the disk he had given me from my pocket, and looked at it.

"I only knew him a short time," I said, "but I liked him. A lot."

"What's that?"

"Something he gave me. A sort of spiritual exercise. Part of one of his magic tricks."

"So we both have gifts to remember him by."

"Yes. I guess we do."

"Thank you, Adam."

"Will you be coming to the ceremony after supper?"

"I think so."

"I'll see you there, then."

My hand was on the door latch when she called after me.

"Adam!"

I turned.

"Yes?"

"If you need anyone, to run an errand or . . . I don't know. I'd like to *help* is all, help find out what happened. I mean it was *Macon*, you know?"

"I know."

"And Adam?"

Her eyes met mine.

"I'm really glad it's you—that you were here, are here."

I nodded, and left for supper.

I WENT STRAIGHT BACK to the Abbot's office, and asked her who she had told about the throwing knife.

"Only Earnest, but I didn't swear him to secrecy. And of course the healers know."

"So it's all over the Abbey by now."

"I'm afraid so. Is that important?"

"Honestly, I don't know."

I WAS glad for the silence at supper.

I welcomed the chance to be with others, and to be left to my thoughts at the same time. A combination of solitude and community.

The somber mood of Stonesday had been replaced, or perhaps amplified, by the community's grief at Brother Macon's death—and by horror that it had been at the hand of someone in the community.

I would have liked to have spent the time putting my thoughts in order, but my mind wouldn't rest. It bounced from one thought to another, without any obvious pattern.

Lilith wanted to help.

When Lucky had been facing execution, Bee had wanted to help—to help me find the evidence to save him. She had *insisted* on helping, and without her I probably wouldn't have been able to do it.

But Bee hadn't told me the truth—not all of it. If she had . . .

Could Lilith be lying, too? About what? Her confession about Macon made sense. It explained all sorts of things.

The wine was pretty bland.

Because it was Stonesday.

Lilith's account of her morning made sense. She said she had seen no one, so I couldn't expect anyone to have seen her.

And why would she kill a man she was in love with?

I was stuck in my own world, of course. I only had Lilith's word for her world.

Bee was gone.

And maybe Lucky.

I was lonely.

I hadn't noticed that I was lonely.

And I had just lost another friend. A new friend.

A throwing knife.

There were only two throwers at the Abbey, as far as we knew.

Only one as far as *I* knew. I had seen the Abbot throw. I had only the Abbot's word that Lilith could throw.

And the Abbot had a motive.

Though I only had Lilith's word for that.

The worlds were multiplying.

So many worlds.

Each of us alone in our own.

The killer had to take the knives from the cabinet sometime between the last time I saw Lilith holding them and the snow on Thursday night.

A throwing knife could still be used to stab someone. It would be awkward, but not impossible.

I wasn't up to this task.

Brine must have known that I wasn't up to this task.

What did Brine mean by giving me that riddle?

What had I missed in the poem about the tree by the stream?

What was the one thing I could experience without my own categories?

This food was practically tasteless.

It was Stonesday.

I was about to take part in a Stonesday ceremony, at an Abbey.

I had been drinking with a monk on Stoneseve.

Macon.

Macon was dead.

Macon could have let the killer in himself.

He would have had to leave them standing at the door while he walked around the firmament to stand behind the tray.

Unless the knife wasn't thrown.

Would he have let Lilith in, if she asked?

Lilith could persuade almost anyone to do anything.

He wouldn't have *had* to let the Abbot in.

Lilith wouldn't kill anyone, would she? Would the Abbot?

I was so very lonely.

Chapter 19

"If the well-bred are to remain in our rightful place—if we are to hold on to our wealth and our power—we must make long term plans. We must make the mob both physically and mentally dependent, or face chaos."

Oss Taylor, founder of Mens Dei. Address to the First Committee.

We gathered at dusk and stood in a circle around the space the monks had cleared. We had each been given a candle. This was the one occasion during the year that anyone could hold a flame.

Lilith came and stood beside me.

At the center of the circle there was a patch of loose dirt, about the shape of a coffin. It had been smoothed, and then a quite abstract sketch of Joshua had been scratched into the surface.

It was an elegant approach. Some churches used ice sculptures. Some packed a mold full of dirt, then removed it, leaving a figure. Some were even more elaborate. But there was a certain power in this simple image, scratched on the surface of loose soil.

And something about it tugged at my memory.

Something Brother Macon had said—not about soil exactly . . .

But I couldn't place it, and the ceremony was about to begin.

The Abbot lit her candle, then handed it to Brother Earnest, who stood beside her. She then picked up one of the stones and took a step forward into the circle.

She recited the scripture from memory.

"It was at sunset that they found him, praying alone on a barren hill, and they made a circle around him, having brought with them their stones.

"And he said to them, 'What has brought you here at this time, and in this private place? I am in the marketplace every day. Are you ashamed of this you do, that you do it in secret?'

"And they said unto him, 'You have committed heresy against God and against your faith. You have made yourself equal to God. And for that you must die.'

"And he said, 'Have I labored so long among you, and still you do not understand?'

"And he turned and knelt before them, and began again to pray. And one who was a leader among them hurled the first stone, which knocked him to the ground. And the rest likewise until there was a pile of stones so large that no part of him could be seen.

"And they posted a guard, lest his followers dig him out and he might be revived. And they kept the guard for three nights and two days."

The Abbot then carried her stone to the center of the circle, and gently placed it on the figure scratched in the dirt.

"This," she said, "you suffered for me."

When she returned to her place in the circle, she took her candle back. Then Brother Earnest lit his candle from hers, handed it to the monk next to him, and stepped forward to place his stone next to the one she had left.

"This," he said, "you suffered for me."

Then the monk standing next to Earnest did the same, and the monk standing next to him, and so on around the circle, each in their turn, and each intoning, "This you suffered for me."

It was dark by the time we finished, standing in a circle around a great pile of stones, each holding a candle against the night.

The Abbot then blew out her candle, and placed it on the ground in front of her, the wick pointing toward the pile of stones.

"And so was his light put out."

The rest of us did the same, as one, and echoed the words together.

"And so was his light put out."

"Let us join hands," the Abbot said, "and meditate on his death."

So we did. I took the hand of the monk to my left, and Lilith took mine.

Lilith walked with me back to our rooms, clinging to my arm. It wasn't clear why—because it was dark, because it was cold, for comfort?

When we got to her door she gave me a chaste peck on the cheek and disappeared inside.

I entered my own room exhausted from the stress of the day, pulled my shoes off, and collapsed on the bed.

As tired as I was, I was afraid I wouldn't be able to sleep until I'd put my thoughts in order.

I woke with the sun shining through the window, still in my clothes, muscles aching. I apparently hadn't moved all night.

I hauled myself out of bed and lumbered to the shower. I undressed while it warmed up. By the time I had shaved and brushed my teeth I had to wipe the steam off the mirror.

And I hadn't been under the shower for more than thirty seconds when it turned ice cold.

There was nothing gradual about it.

I knocked the nozzle sideways, yanked the valve off, and stood wet and shivering on the hard tile. Then I pulled a towel off the rack and rubbed myself briskly, trying to warm up.

It didn't help.

I dressed and hurried down to the common room, where I fortified myself with a hot cup of tea and sat as close to the fire as I could bear.

Once there, I began to form a plan for the day.

I decided I would concentrate on one person at a time, until I could eliminate her from suspicion. The obvious candidates were Lilith and the Abbot.

I would start with Lilith. She was the only one who could leave the Abbey once I cleared her. Get away to where it was safe. And when I had eliminated her as a suspect I would move on to the Abbot. By the time I had eliminated both of them, I might have good reason to suspect someone else.

But for now I would concentrate on Lilith.

———

After breakfast I went straight to the Abbot's office, in order to catch her before the Sunday service.

She looked up from her Bible as I entered.

"Pastor."

"Sorry to bother you. I just wanted to tell you that I won't be at the service this morning. My apologies for that, too, but I'll be busy investigating the . . . the death."

"I'm as anxious to get this settled as you are, Pastor. And you won't miss much. When a Sunday falls on one of the Deathdays, we observe a minimal service, as a symbolic mourning. Of course, today it won't just be symbolic."

"And I wonder if I could be given access to the Master Wright's workroom until this is cleared up?"

"Yes. Of course."

She shot me a wry smile.

"Not, you understand, for Pastor Kinde, on a dubious fact-finding mission for his local presbytery. But for the ecclesiastical judge helping us clear up the murder of Brother Macon, *that* I can do."

She motioned me forward.

"Stick out your hand."

I did, the same way I had on the first day.

She held her Bible up in the same way as well.

"That's done. Anything else?"

"I'm going to need some time with you after the service, if you wouldn't mind."

"I'll be here, in my office."

I set off down the path, and passed the chapel just as the gong rang for Sunday morning service.

I had no trouble entering the research facility, and when I got to the door of Brother Macon's workroom I found Brother Earnest standing guard.

"Brother Earnest! Have you been here all night?"

He grinned.

"I had a couple of the other monks take shifts. There's hardly ever anyone else around this floor at night. Brother Macon was the only one with a bed in his room. Most everyone else is back in their cell before it's very late."

"And you're taking the day shifts?"

"The Abbot has given your investigation top priority. So I wanted to be here when there were likely to be others around, just to make sure."

"I appreciate that."

He opened the door for me, and stood aside.

"Let me know if there's anything I can do to help."

THE DOOR CLOSED BEHIND ME, and I was back in Brother Macon's world.

The scent of coffee was stale, but everything else was the same.

I stood in the doorway for a moment, imagining him standing behind the little tray.

I pantomimed throwing a knife—hoping that there wouldn't be enough room—but there was. It could easily have been done that way.

I moved around the firmament, and crouched to examine the floor behind the stand and tray.

I couldn't find anything instructive there at all.

His Bible was sitting on the drawing table in the corner.

I picked it up.

Perhaps.

It was a possibility anyway.

I crossed to the little tray again. With the body gone, I could pantomime someone reaching around him from behind with a knife.

It didn't seem likely.

I had a deep wish that I knew what the hell I was doing.

As I turned to leave, I noticed the box that the sketch of the *M* of hearts had been hidden under on our first visit.

I picked it up. There was a drawing under it.

The *M* of hearts.

He had put it back.

So I had been right. He'd had some way of making me choose that card.

I'd never know how, now.

I put the sketch back under the box, but then another thought struck me.

I picked up another box, then another and another.

The third one I picked up had a folded paper underneath.

I unfolded it.

A sketch. The *R* of diamonds.

I stopped searching after I found five sketches hidden in the room.

He had kept his entire workroom constantly prepared for that trick. Whatever card I had chosen, he knew exactly which object to tell me to pick up.

The clever scoundrel.

And that gave me an idea, only it wasn't quite conscious yet. There was something about that trick that might have some vague connection with his death. Not directly, maybe, but somehow.

If I could just put my finger on it.

Chapter 20

"Robert Smith combined religious devotion with inspired engineering design. Oss Taylor funded his research and brought him into Mens Dei, where he developed the prototype for the 'firmaments,' the 'monkstone algorithm,' and the resultant 'spirit channeling.'"

Rita Willnard, *Mens Dei and the "Tribulation Crisis"*

BROTHER EARNEST WAS STILL STANDING guard outside the door when I left.

Still smiling.

I needed to talk to the Abbot next, but I didn't think the service would be over. On a whim, I strolled around the walkway to Day Seven, the meditation room.

Since the monks were all at the service, I had it to myself. It was on the side of the building away from the entrance, and unlike the other rooms it had a large stained-glass window.

There was no altar, since no one preached here—and since no one came here to have their Bible blessed.

The chairs and kneelers formed a circle in the center of the room. I seated myself, and tried once more to pray.

Nothing. My words were just words with no one to hear them.

I thought about what Pastor Dean had said at our last session.

What exactly had changed? Was the change in God, or in me?

And the poem he had given me. I ran over it again in my mind.

Blessed is one whose faith is in God.
> Who is like a tree planted by the stream.
> Its leaves remain green when the heat comes.
> It bears fruit in the year of drought.

If I was like a tree planted by the stream, then what was the stream?

Probably God.

So my leaves would remain green even though it was hot, because I'm planted by the stream.

And I would bear fruit in the year of . . .

But in a drought, the stream would be gone.

This *was* a poem about my situation. A poem about God being gone. But how did it help?

And what was the one thing I could experience without my own categories?

I had imagined God in front and a little above me. Pastor Dean thought that was important.

Maybe it was like the duck and the rabbit. Maybe I needed a new category. Maybe I just had to look for God in a different way.

Maybe.

But I didn't know how to do that.

And I was exhausted by it all.

I fell into a sort of trance, too tired to think. Just sitting there in the quiet room, bathed in the colored light from the window, breathing and being, without thought or emotion.

Resting, for the first time since I'd lost Bee.

WHEN THE SERVICE was over I stood outside the chapel, waiting for the Abbot.

She was the last one out. As she approached she reached out for Macon's Bible.

"Thanks. I'll take care of it."

I didn't hand it to her.

"I'm not bringing it for cleansing. Not yet."

"Oh?"

"I think I should explain."

"Let's take a walk, then."

We walked along the path toward the Abbey, then turned down the path I had arrived by that first day. It was noticeably warmer than it had been then, and the sunshine gleamed on the snow.

"I need your help, so I'm going to fill you in on what I think you need to know, even though technically you have to be one of my suspects."

"I'm glad to hear the word 'technically.'"

"I don't have many options. So far, not one suspect seems like a killer to me."

"So?"

"So I've decided to take you one at a time. I'm hoping that by the time I've cleared all three of you—"

"Meaning me, Sister Edith, and Brother Earnest?"

"Maybe by the time you're all cleared, another, more believable suspect will turn up."

"So you consider all of us to be 'technical'."

I nodded.

"Today, I'm concentrating on Lilith—on Sister Edith."

"Really? I expected to be first."

"Why?"

"Because I'm more likely. You have to suspect your friend and me because we're both throwers. You have to suspect me and Earnest because we both had access to the room where it was done. I'm the only one in both categories. So why start with Sister Edith?"

I'd already told her too much. I couldn't explain that Lilith could leave the abbey to safety without explaining why I thought she might be in danger. And I wasn't ready to tell anyone that I knew about the second missing knife.

So I dissembled.

"You're probably right, but I have some idea how to proceed with Sister Edith."

"And that is?"

"I questioned her, and she made some claims that I can check up on."

"Are you going to share them with me?"

"That's the point. She claims that she and Brother Macon were attracted to each other."

"Preposterous."

"She doesn't claim that they ever . . ."

"It's still nonsense."

"They *are* both human."

"I'm not saying that Brother Macon was immune to such attractions, just that if he *were* attracted to her she would never have known about it."

"Right. And based on my experience of him, I would tend to agree. The problem is that her story explains some things that didn't make sense before I heard it. So I'd like to *prove* that she's telling the truth or that she's *not*."

"And how do you propose to do that?"

"She claims they were exchanging words regularly since they met. When I asked to see them, she said she couldn't send them to me because she hadn't kept them. Said they were too 'embarrassing'."

"Convenient."

"That thought occurred to me, as well. I don't know the protocols of Abbey life, but I understand that the Abbot has enormous authority within the Abbey."

"It's true, though it's not my way to use that authority any more than I have to."

I held up Macon's Bible.

She shook her head.

"I certainly wouldn't violate the privacy of one who was chosen."

"Can you hear me out, before deciding?"

"I can listen, but don't expect it to make a difference."

"First of all, he's dead now, and it can't make that much difference to him."

She shook her head. I continued.

"Second, it's on the request of an ecclesiastical judge, trying to find his killer."

She shook her head again. I pressed on.

"Third, I only want to see a specific exchange, which could exonerate an innocent suspect, or incriminate a guilty one."

This time she didn't shake her head. I decided to take a chance.

"Fourth, Sister Edith—"

"You can call her Lilith if you want."

"Fourth, *Lilith* claims that somewhere in those words Brother Macon incriminates you."

She looked a little startled at that. She paused, then shook her head more vehemently than before.

"Now you're trying to muddy my thinking with personal agendas. You forget I'm a fleecer. I'm not likely to fall for that."

"Actually, *telling* you that was a kind of fleece on my part."

She chuckled at that.

"Would I be *afraid* to let you see them, you mean?"

I finished making my case.

"My final point is that, given everything I've already said, letting me see those words would hardly set a precedent. Just how many times do you expect this set of conditions to occur? And even if they did, wouldn't it be wise to make the same exception again?"

She actually considered that. After a moment she nodded.

"Okay. You've convinced me."

She reached for the Bible.

This time I let her take it.

It only took her a moment to unlock Macon's Bible.

We had reached the end of the path, and were standing on the edge of the road where Brine's angel had dropped me off almost a week before.

Where I had first seen Lilith, walking away from me.

I stood beside the Abbot, watching carefully. I didn't want to give her the opportunity to remove anything from the exchange.

She found it, and opened it.

Lilith had been right about the correspondence itself. They had written almost daily since they had met at that conference.

But the words themselves were strange. They consisted mostly of small talk—gossip about other members of the conference, about the politics surrounding theological debates, about the food at the conference and what had been said at various meetings.

There was absolutely nothing personal in them. Certainly nothing embarrassing. No reason at all to remove them.

And there was nothing at all about Macon's life at the Abbey. No mention of the Abbot or anyone else.

The only exception to that came toward the very end, when Macon said that he had some friends at the Abbey that she would like.

That was it. Nothing more.

The Abbot's hand poised over the surface of the Bible.

"Anything else you need to see?"

"Nothing."

She waved it closed and the surface was blank again except for Macon's name.

"Well," she said, "that was hardly worth our lengthy debate."

"I don't know. It clears you of her accusations at least, and it tells me she was lying about their correspondence—even if it doesn't tell me why."

I glanced up and down the road.

"Where does this lead?"

"That way it wanders down toward the local village. The other way it leads to the local holder's estate. I take a stroll up there most mornings, early. There's a really nice view toward the top. Can I ask *you* a question?"

"I think you deserve at least one."

"What did Lilith claim those words would say about me?"

"She said you had done something wrong, and Macon was trying to decide whether to confront you about it."

"A rather nasty little lie, given the circumstances."

"She also said she didn't believe you had killed him."

"Still, it paints a nice little picture. The confrontation, an argument, things get out of hand . . ."

"And then what? You walk around the firmament to the door, turn and throw the knife at him? The knife that you just happened to have brought with you?"

"But did she know it was a thrown knife when she told you this story?"

"I don't know. She did if she was the killer."

"But then she would know that the story she was spinning wouldn't fit the evidence. And if she wasn't the killer—"

"—she wouldn't have any reason to make me suspect you instead."

We turned our steps back toward the Abbey, giving me the same view that I'd had on the day I arrived. The sign Lilith had stopped to read was still there, beside the path.

But Lilith was missing from that scene.

And something else was missing as well. Had been missing that very first day. I couldn't think what it was, except that it should have been there, and wasn't.

Chapter 21

"It is quite clear, even to a traditionalist like myself, that the media most watched by the devout has become self-serving and full of lies. This will do us no good in the end, and may even lead to tyranny."

Michael Kinde, ancestor of Adam Kinde

AFTER LUNCH I hiked to the hermitage for my next counseling session. I wasn't in the mood for that, but I hadn't done anything to cancel it either, and it seemed the height of rudeness to not keep an appointment with a hermit.

When I got to the fork in the trail, I had another thought. So I hiked down to the hermitage, and knocked on the door.

"Come."

I stuck my head in the doorway.

"Would you mind if I skipped our session today?"

He smiled.

"Of course I would. You are very pleasant company. But I'm sure you have a good reason."

"It's just that . . ."

I stepped inside.

"I guess I can tell you—in confidence of course."

"I promise. What is it?"

"I'm supposed to be finding out who killed Brother Macon."

"Pressing business. I understand."

"Only it's more pressing than that. He was killed with a throwing knife. No one else knows this, but I visited the Abbot's throwing clearing, and there are *two* knives missing."

"So you're worried there may be a second victim soon."

"Exactly."

"So why are you standing here, wasting time?"

I hiked back to the fork in the road and took the other path, up toward the cemetery.

About halfway there I came across the bench that Lilith had described.

I sat down, and surveyed the terrain. It was just possible that she was telling the truth about hiking up to the bench, but not the whole truth. I didn't know the Abbey grounds well enough to be certain that there was no way to Macon's work-room from the path to the cemetery.

The hill dropped off steeply at the downhill side of the trail, and the brush grew thick on the slope. I couldn't imagine her getting through that to get back to the research facility.

I walked further up the trail, until it curved back on itself on its way to the top of the hill. I couldn't find any place with a passable route downhill.

I retraced my steps and gave the same inspection to the slope between the bench and the path to the hermitage. It was the same. I was pretty sure she couldn't have gotten to Macon from anywhere on that part of the trail.

I headed down from the fork toward the Abbey, but about halfway there I stopped.

There it was. A slight slope with almost no growth, and below that a faintly visible footpath.

I had no trouble getting down to the path, and no trouble following it.

It took me straight to the research facility.

I took the path by the chapel back to the abbey, dreading what I knew I had to do next.

Lilith was just leaving her room when I got there.

"Adam! What's wrong?"

"I'm sorry, Lilith, but I have to search your room."

A mixture of hurt and anger flashed across her face, then her jaw tightened.

"I don't think so."

"I really am sorry. But Brother Macon is dead, and it's my job to find out who did it."

Her eyes flashed.

"And searching my room is really going to help? Are you sure you don't just want an excuse to go through my underclothes?"

"That's not fair. Or very mature."

"*You know* I had nothing to do with dear Macon's death."

"We'll talk about that when I've finished. Right now—"

She stepped in front of me.

"No!"

"What are you afraid I'll find?"

"That's not the point."

I paused, gave her a moment, then lowered my voice. I think some of my weariness came through.

"Believe me, Lilith. I wouldn't be doing this if I didn't absolutely have to. But I do have to. And you're not going to stop me."

She glared at me.

"I will never forgive you for this, Adam."

"I know."

I stepped past her and opened the door.

She hung about, just outside, while I went methodically through her things. There was nothing unusual in her suitcase, except for a small golden sculpture. It appeared to be an abstract model of a bug, about the size of my palm.

I was pretty sure it was the same object Macon had been working on when I first entered his door.

I turned, and held it up to Lilith.

She just glared at me.

I met her eyes, and continued to hold it up.

Finally she relented.

"Macon's gift to me. You brought it yourself."

I put it back and closed the suitcase.

Then I went through the rest of the room. I was really only looking for one thing, but I didn't want to overlook any evidence I hadn't anticipated.

There was nothing to be found. And I was thorough. I had really expected that the other knife would be in the suitcase or under the mattress if it was there at all, but it wasn't.

I finally collapsed into the chair, and gave a sigh of defeat.

Lilith raised an eyebrow at me.

"Satisfied?"

I didn't know whether I felt more relieved or embarrassed. But the job needed to be completed.

"Come on in and sit down. I need to ask you a few questions."

She sat on the bed.

"I thought we already did this."

"Yes. Well, you lied."

"That's what brought this about?"

"What could you expect?"

"So how did I lie?"

"You lied about your correspondence with Brother Macon. You lied about your relationship with him. You lied about his accusations concerning the Abbot—"

"—and I lied about how good I am at throwing, or have you discovered that one yet?"

"The Abbot saw through you immediately. Apparently your performance was only good enough to fool *me*."

"I thought so, though it was good of her to let me get away with it. There wasn't anybody dead at the time, you know. It was just good manners not to show up my host."

"And the other lies?"

"Macon and I became friends at that conference, but just friends—on his side, at least. I really did have quite a crush. But I didn't admit that to myself. So when I scheduled my retreat I scheduled it here, telling myself that it would be good to see a friend.

"When I arrived, however, I realized almost immediately how strong my crush was, and I didn't trust myself not to do something foolish. I arranged to take my meals in my room so I wouldn't meet him there, and then I just kept my distance— except for arranging to exchange gifts, which I couldn't resist.

"But when he was killed I realized I had practically implicated myself. I had hidden the fact that I was good with a throwing knife, and I had made it clear that we knew each other well enough to exchange gifts, but for some reason I had avoided him ever since I came. It would all look very suspicious.

"I panicked. I tried to invent a story that would make all my strange behavior make sense. I tried to turn your suspicions away from me toward the Abbot—whom I actually *do* suspect, if you want to know. And I'm afraid I assumed you'd be easy to fool because of our history. It was all very stupid, and all very wrong of me.

"And this time," she said, "that's the truth."

She paused, then gave me a rueful smile.

"I guess I deserved all of this. I'm sorry I was such a pig about it."

"I'm sorry I had to do it."

"Oh! There's one more thing! I found someone who saw me going off to meditate. And coming back as well."

LILITH LED me to the common room, and to the ancient monk sitting in the corner.

His window had a clear view of the path leading to the cemetery.

"Brother Rupert," she said, "I'd like you to meet Adam. He's a friend of mine—and the ecclesiastical judge."

The old fellow smiled up at me.

"It's true," he said.

His voice, coming from within all those wrinkles, was stronger and more assured than I would have expected. But he still smelled like an old man.

"What's true?"

"I saw her. On Stonesday."

"Do you remember when?"

"Right after breakfast, going up the hill. She came from the retreat cabins at the back."

"And you were sitting here all morning?"

"*Every* morning." There was a twinkle in his eye. "It gives the others a sense of youth and vitality to see me."

"And when did she come back down?"

"Just as we were going in, to lunch."

Lilith beamed at me.

"So I'm in the clear, right?"

Chapter 22

"Smith's inventions were to provide the economic fulcrum which made possible the unification of the various denominations preceding the Council of Columbia. But they also made it possible to address the climate issue head on."

Rita Willnard, *Mens Dei and the "Tribulation Crisis"*

SHE WASN'T, of course. In the clear.

There was still the path halfway up to the hermitage. The old monk could have seen her hike up the trail until she was out of sight, and she could still have followed that path to meet Macon. And even if they weren't lovers, she could have persuaded him to let her in.

But I was at a loss how to prove she'd done that, or how to prove she hadn't.

I wandered up the trail again, mulling the problem over.

I passed the point where I could look back and see the Abbey.

A little later I passed the slope down to the foot path.

I kept hiking until I reached the fork in the trail.

I took the trail to the hermitage and knocked on the door.

"Come."

Pastor Dean looked up from his game of Shadow.

"I thought you were taking a day off?"

"I hit a dead end."

"And?"

"I don't know. I guess I thought I might as well see if you could still do our session."

He motioned me to my chair, and got up to prepare the tea.

"Have you had time to think about the poem?"

"I have, actually."

"Any conclusions?"

"Only that it really is about my problem. The tree is planted by the stream. I'm the tree, and the stream is God. Then the drought comes. But that would mean the stream dries up—God goes away."

"Very good. You're at least halfway there. What about my other question?"

"What part of God's creation can I experience without my own categories? I have no idea."

"None at all?"

"Why does this all have to be riddles, anyway?"

"It doesn't. This is just one way of doing it—the way I prefer."

"Because?"

"One of the difficulties—maybe the greatest difficulty—in spiritual counseling is that we humans are experts at fooling ourselves. Knowledge, real knowledge, is a mixture of language, behavior, experience, and understanding. But we can easily mimic the first two without the others."

"We can act and talk like we've experienced or understood something, even if we haven't?"

"Right. Can you see where I'm headed?"

"You use riddles because they require understanding or experience to unravel. They keep me from fooling myself into thinking I've solved my problem when I haven't."

"Satisfied?"

"For now, but I still don't have the slightest idea about your riddles."

"Let's think about the second one. We'll start with something you can only know through your own categories. How would you describe your experience of a duck?"

"As being completely different from my experience of a rabbit."

He laughed at that.

"Sorry. Bad example if you've been talking to the Abbot. Let's make it a sparrow."

"Well, it's a bird, obviously."

"Which is one of your categories."

"It has feathers."

"Another category."

"It can fly—okay. I get nothing but a combination of my own categories."

"So do you have any idea, at all, what it is like to *be* a sparrow? What a sparrow *is*—not in your creation, but in God's?"

"None, really."

"How about a mouse?"

"No."

"Or any of God's creations. A cat? A tree? An angel?"

That was when it hit me.

"Wait a minute. Could I . . . Sorry, but I need . . . I need to talk to your guardian angel."

It was a truly beautiful day.

She wasn't on the trail back to the Abbey, and she wasn't in the common room.

The Abbot hadn't seen her. She wasn't in the chapel.

There was no answer when I knocked at her door, and I certainly wasn't going to open it again, after the trouble I'd created searching her room.

I was trying to think where else she could be when I heard a knocking, and looked up the path.

It was Lilith, knocking on *my* door.

I hurried up to meet her and invited her in.

She sensed the change in my mood and gave me a questioning glance.

"Good news!" I blurted. "You really are in the clear."

She looked confused.

"Yes. The old monk . . ."

"That helped, of course. But unfortunately there's a path, further up the trail, that leads back to the research facility."

"So you still—"

"I still needed absolute proof of your innocence. And I found it."

"How?"

"I should have thought of it sooner. The hermit's guardian angel is constantly on guard along that path, keeping everyone who passes from disrespecting 'the solitude of the hermit.' And there's no one more literal and exact than an angel."

"It remembered me."

"It not only saw you passing both ways, it could say exactly when. It could even vouch that you were at the bench the entire morning."

"So you don't have to suspect me anymore."

"Better than that. You can leave the Abbey."

She squeezed my hand, looking a little hurt.

"You want me to leave?"

I squeezed back.

"I don't, to be honest. But there's a killer among us, Lilith, and we don't know for sure whether Brother Macon will be the only victim. I want you to be safe. Even more than I want your company."

"That's very sweet. And romantic. But I do need to stay for the funeral."

"I really think you should leave first thing in the morning."

She stepped forward, and put her lips on mine. It brought back memories. When she finally stepped back I was at a loss.

She took my hand again.

"Still want me to go?"

I didn't. I really didn't.

"You have to. You really do."

She stepped forward again. I felt my arm going around that familiar waist, smelled the familiar sweetness of her breath. I pulled her closer, pressing her against me.

But something was wrong.

It brought back memories, but not the memories I wanted.

I pulled back, and looked into those eyes I had known so well, so long ago, and they weren't the eyes I wanted to see.

They weren't Bee's eyes.

She smiled, and it wasn't Bee's smile.

"What's wrong?"

"Nothing—with you. But . . ."

Then she stepped back and nodded, knowingly.

"I'm not her."

I shrugged.

"And I'm not over her."

Her eyes were sad, but she kissed her fingertips, then touched them to my lips.

"Goodbye, Adam."

And she left.

IT WAS IRONIC, really.

That wasn't the first time I'd kissed Lilith, of course, but it was the first I'd kissed her *this* time—at the Abbey.

I kissed her, and then I sent her away.

The first time I'd kissed Bee had been on that rainy night in the parsonage, just hours before Tho attacked her. We had kissed, and it had been absolutely clear that we were meant for each other.

We'd talked until late, then sat quietly together, my arm around her, the weight of her head on my chest, the scent of her hair in my head, the pounding rain outside the window, and I don't think she would have ever left.

But then I had realized that Bee was a Human—an infidel. That her logo was fake, that she had misled me. And I was a pastor who couldn't marry an infidel.

All of which I regretted, but not as much as I regretted what I had done next.

I had, for all intents and purposes, sent her away.

And now I had sent Lilith away, because she wasn't Bee.

Maybe *that* was my type. Women I sent away.

The Abbot found me in the common room, waiting for supper, and pulled me aside.

"Can I ask another favor?"

"You can certainly *ask*."

"How *generous*. Do you really still need a guard on Macon's door?"

"Why?"

"It's just that I could use Earnest for other duties, but he seems determined to be the guard as long as there is one."

I thought about it.

"There's only the three of us who could get in, anyway. And no one else seems to have even tried."

"So I can tell him to come in for supper?"

"Sure."

"Your friend tells me she's leaving in the morning."

"Lilith? That's good news. I'd just as soon have at least one person out of danger."

"Out of danger?"

"There's still a killer at the Abbey."

"And you've decided it's not her?"

"She didn't tell you about that?"

"No. Just said she was leaving."

"I finally proved she couldn't have done it. The angel at the hermitage vouched for her whereabouts during the entire morning."

"The angel? It actually *cooperated*? Very resourceful of you."

"I'm pretty proud of that, myself."

"That leaves me and Earnest."

"Until someone else turns up."

"Well, I have work to do."

"You're not eating?"

"I'll have something at my desk. No rest for the wicked."

She left through the front door.

The room grew more crowded as the community gathered for supper, until finally the doors opened. Everyone began moving toward the dining room.

Brother Earnest joined me, a bit out of breath.

"Don't worry," he smiled, "I let her in before I left."

"Let who in?"

His smile vanished.

"Sister Edith. She said you wanted her to fetch something from the room."

Chapter 23

I SLIPPED on a patch of ice just outside the research facility, lost my balance and crashed, shoulder first, into the door.

My Bible tumbled and slid off the path, half burying itself in the snow.

It was what I got for trying to run in that kind of weather. Luckily, I had left my walking stick in my room, or I might have skewered myself on it.

I lay there for a moment, catching my breath while the

initial shot of pain subsided, then very carefully climbed to my feet, one hand on the door to steady myself.

Once up, I made my way to the edge of the path, and managed to stoop down without too much discomfort to retrieve my Bible.

I let myself in and went straight to Macon's workroom.

I opened the door, and stepped inside.

There was no sign of her.

My first thought was that she had already gotten whatever she came for, and left.

Then I noticed the smell—the same metallic scent that had been in the air when I had first seen Macon's body.

I moved slowly around the firmament until I could see the floor where Macon had died.

Only now it was Lilith.

She was in roughly the same position as Macon had been. She was on her left side—apparently crawling in a different direction, but her feet were not far from where Macon's had been. The second knife was in her shoulder.

I opened my Bible and prayed for a healer, then crouched down beside her to feel for a pulse. I had forgotten about my own fall, and when the pain came, I ignored it.

She was dead.

I polished the surface of my Bible and held it in front of her mouth to be sure.

Nothing.

I was still crouched there when the healers arrived. Two of them coaxed me to my feet and got me into a chair by Macon's drawing board.

After a time I realized that someone was talking to me.

". . . take the body?"

I looked up to see the Abbot, standing beside me. She looked worried.

"Are you all right?"

I looked back at the healers, crouched around Lilith, and suddenly shivered.

The Abbot was still talking.

"Pastor?"

I shivered again, and the fog dissipated a little.

"Sorry. What were you saying?"

"Are you okay?"

I nodded.

"I will be."

"The healers want to know if they can take the body back to our morgue."

It took me a moment to process that.

"Yeah. I don't see why . . . Yeah."

She took a step toward the healers, and my fog abruptly lifted.

"Wait! These healers. Do you know them?"

"Know them? They're part of the staff at the Abbey. They're not monks themselves, but they're part of our community."

"For how long? Have any of them arrived recently?"

"They've all been here longer than I have. Why?"

"Nothing. It's okay. They can take her."

* * *

THE LAST TIME I saw Bee alive she was sprinting down an alley toward me, a look of grim determination on her face.

Tho had aimed a police rod at her back, and an arc of bright blue light had knocked her off her feet.

The healers had appeared almost immediately. It took two of them to drag me away from her. They helped me lean against the wall of a building, and one stayed with me while the other retrieved my stick.

A third knelt over Bee. It didn't take him long before the ambulance turned black and they took her body away.

And I never saw her again.

There was no record of an ambulance going out that night. I never discovered whether the healers who took her were really even healers at all.

She just vanished.

Dennis had said that she was a Human, and apparently Humans retrieve their own dead.

"BETTER?"

The Abbot poured more cocoa into my mug. She had taken me in hand after my foggy responses over Lilith's body, walked me back to her office, ordered hot cocoa and grilled cheese sandwiches from the monks in the kitchen, and sat me down at her table.

"Yes," I said. "I think so."

"This is my comfort food. A bit too appetizing for a Death-day, but under the circumstances I think it's warranted."

"It's very good. Very sustaining."

"I apologize, by the way, for thinking you were being alarmist when you wanted Lilith to leave."

"You were right, given what you knew. I had visited the knife-throwing clearing, you see, and I had found *two* knives missing. I hadn't told anyone, because I didn't want the killer to know that I knew. And Lilith was the only person who could leave, could get to safety."

"And that was the only reason? I thought there might be more."

"Yes. Well, there might have been. Actually, I think I may have made the mistake you warned me against there."

"*I* warned you against?"

"Fooling myself into believing what I wanted to believe."

"I see. That makes this more difficult for you, then. But you didn't really anticipate that she was the next target?"

"I haven't a clue, really, about this whole situation. At least it seems the killing may be over. Except—is there somewhere we can lock up the rest of those knives?"

"Of course. I should have thought of that. I should have realized that was where the killer got it."

"We're all amateurs at this."

We sat in silence for a while, sipping and eating.

Then I had a thought.

"I suppose I have to ask you where you went after you left me in the common room."

"I came back to the office to work. And I didn't see anyone until I got the word from the healers, so I suspect you won't be able to find anyone who saw me."

"And Brother Earnest was definitely there. He let her in."

"I just don't believe Earnest would kill anyone. *And* I've never seen him throw a knife."

"I'll need to ask him more specifically what she said when she talked him into letting her in."

"Should I send for him?"

"It *would* be best to talk to him while his memory is still fresh. But I'm done in. Let's leave it to morning."

I OVERSLEPT the next morning and missed breakfast.

I wasn't as stiff or sore as I would have expected, given my fall.

As soon as I was dressed I headed straight for the clearing. The only tracks in the snow at the entrance were mine, from my previous visit.

I opened the shed, and it was just as I had left it. Two knives missing—no more and no less.

I gathered up all the others and wrapped them in the towel I had brought from my room, then carried them back to the Abbey, and the Abbot's office.

She was there, sitting at her desk, absorbed in something she was reading on her Bible.

I put my bundle down on her table, and took a seat.

She came to a stopping place, and looked up.

"What's this?"

"The rest of the knives. Do you have a safe place to keep them?"

She got up, rummaged in a drawer, and pulled out a rolled up piece of leather, tied together with a cord. She brought that over to the table and unrolled it.

It was a storage case for knives—probably for those exact knives—with nine leather pockets.

"I should have kept them in this all along. Leaving them in the shed was convenient, but lazy. And also dangerous."

She took them one at a time, slid each into its pocket, then stepped back and looked at me.

"Seven. Right?"

"Yes."

"So just the two missing."

"Right."

She rolled it up, tied the cord, then stepped to a door built into the shelves on one wall. She waved at its lock plate, opened the door, and put the knives inside.

"I'm the only one who can open that—not even Earnest has

access. So if one goes missing you'll have to suspect me, not him."

"I do hope that doesn't happen."

"Not as much as I do."

"Do you have time to talk?"

"What's on your mind?"

"This may sound odd. I'm stumped by this whole affair. I'll question Earnest about what Lilith said today, and I'll probably visit the morgue, to examine Lilith's body for anything that might tell me something. But I don't expect either of those to get me anywhere."

"You've hit a dead end. And you want to talk it over with one of your main suspects?"

"With one of my only two suspects, actually. The one who also happens to be a fleecer."

"You want to know how a fleecer would approach the problem."

"Something like that."

"Well, I'd probably make a list of questions first."

"Like 'who did it'?"

She laughed.

"Probably more detailed than that."

I opened my Bible.

"Question one," I said. "What did Lilith want to get from Brother Macon's workroom?"

"Any ideas?"

"She did exchange gifts with Macon—they asked me to deliver them. Maybe she wanted to retrieve hers?"

"It's a possibility."

"So she either found it, or she didn't. And either her killer took it, or—or it will be among her things at the morgue."

"Worth checking."

"So question two. How did the killer know she would be there, at that time?"

"Well, *if* it was Earnest—and I've already said I don't think it was—he was the one who let her in. If it was me . . . I can't guess how I would have known."

"Maybe he told you, when you sent word to come to supper."

"You can ask him about that, when you talk to him."

"Right. And of course the biggest question—question three —is 'why?' Why would anyone want to kill both Macon and Lilith? What did the two of them have in common?"

"They both attended that conference. That's how they met. Something about that?"

"Maybe. Or maybe it has something to do with those chains."

I thought she looked a little wary when I said that, but she nodded anyway.

"You mean the ones like mine and our hermit's."

"Yes. What do they mean?"

"Aside from the rather clumsy reference to the Holy Duality?"

"Yes. Only four of you have them, and two of you are dead."

"What can I tell you? Macon enjoyed making them. He gave them to friends. I don't actually know that we were the only four he gave them to."

"And *question* four—if it wasn't you or Brother Earnest, then how did the killer get in?"

"Unless Macon let them in."

"There's always that. This is just taking me in circles."

"That happens to fleecers all the time. Our usual advice is to give the problem a rest. Think about other things for a while, and let your deep word and spirit work on the chaos until they bring something new to light."

"My 'deep word and spirit'?"

"The deepest *you*. The you that is directly created by God—the parts of your word and spirit that you aren't even conscious of."

"And that part of me will still work on this puzzle while I'm not even consciously thinking about it?"

"That's our experience."

Chapter 24

I FOUND Brother Earnest on his way back from showing a new retreatant to their room.

For the first time he was not smiling.

"Pastor, I can't tell you how sorry I am. I wasn't supposed to let anyone in. I know that. But the Abbot had just told me not to guard the door anymore, and Sister Edith said you had sent her, and somehow it just didn't even occur to me that she might be—"

I cut him off.

"It's not your fault. Seriously. I have known Sister Edith for a long time, and she can be very persuasive."

"But if I hadn't let her in . . ."

"You don't know that. She might have gotten in another way, or the killer might have done it somewhere else."

He digested that.

"I suppose. Still . . ."

"I need you to tell me exactly what she said to you. Word for word, if you can."

"She showed up right after I received the Abbot's word. I was just leaving the outer door. She seemed to be in a hurry, like she'd been running, all out of breath. She said, 'Quick! Pastor Kinde needs me to get something from Brother Macon's workroom! Can you let me in?'"

He paused, and thought that over.

"I think those were her exact words. At least they're pretty close. I went back in with her and opened the door to the workroom. I probably should have stayed there, but I was hungry, and the supper bell had rung, and she said, 'Don't miss your supper. I can let myself out.' So I came on back, and it never occurred to me that she might be lying, not until I told you."

"What was she doing when you left?"

"She was looking for something. Looking in the boxes on the work-tables, turning things over and looking under them. Just generally searching."

———

BROTHER EARNEST SHOWED me the way to the morgue, which was in the abbey clinic—a building I hadn't visited before.

It was a bare-bones kind of room. Metal sinks and counters bolted to white tiled walls, a stone floor with a drain in the center, and three metal tables in the center of the room.

Two of them were occupied. One held Macon's body, and the other held Lilith.

It was nicer than the morgue in the basement of the police station, where I had examined Will Terren's body and discovered his fake logo. But not much.

The healer, a large man with a bushy mustache and ironic manner, stood ready to answer my questions, but I didn't really have any. So I faked it. And he saw right through me.

"Just to confirm, the death was caused by the knife wound?"

"For which victim, sir?"

"Let's start with the Master Wright."

"You mean Brother Macon?"

"Yes."

"Yes, sir."

"Well?"

"Well what, sir?"

"Was the knife the cause of death?"

"I told you sir. Yes. It was the cause of death."

"And . . ."

"And?"

"Sister Edith?"

"Yes, sir. That is Sister Edith."

"What was her cause of death?"

"A knife wound."

"The same as Brother Macon, then?"

"Quite a coincidence, that."

I deduced from this exchange that the fellow had very little use for outsiders bearing authority, and quite probably had not known Brother Macon well, if at all. It was also clear why he had drawn morgue duty—left to spend his day away from live people.

I circled them both, lifting the blankets that covered them just far enough to inspect the wounds. And learned absolutely nothing.

"Was anything other than clothes found on their bodies?"

"Yes, sir."

He was getting on my nerves.

"Could I please see what was found?"

He nodded to two trays on one of the counters. They each had the robes and underclothes rolled up on one end, and the contents of pockets and other items spread out on the rest of the tray.

I went over Macon's tray first. It contained several items that I assumed he'd used for his magic tricks. I recognized the shell which had fit over the disk in my pocket. There was a hollow metal thumb, painted to match Macon's skin color, a wooden egg with a loop of thread tacked to one end, and several other gadgets that I couldn't categorize at all.

And there was his belt—a single chain of duality links, without any buckle or fastener. He must have forged it to fit so well that he could just pull it up over his hips and it would stay at his waist.

And, of course, there was a necklace holding a polished stone, very much like the one I wore.

The knife that had killed him lay next to the tray, on the counter.

I decided to take the belt with me. It was the only thing there that might be important.

I then turned my attention to Lilith's possessions.

There were fewer of them. Her bracelet, made of tiny duality links, had one ordinary link connecting it to her stone— the rough teardrop of the Joshuan order. A gold finger ring, studded with ruby stones, which I had never noticed her wearing. A stylus. There was no sign of her Bible, but it was probably in her room.

If she had gone to Macon's workroom to retrieve her gift, it seemed that she hadn't found it.

The second knife lay next to her tray.

I took the bracelet, for the same reason I had taken Macon's belt.

I thanked the healer and turned to leave.

He called after me.

"I hope your investigation goes well, sir."

"Thank you."

"It's just—we only have the one table left, you see."

I PUT the chains in my room, then found my way to the monks' quarters, and Macon's cell.

It was small, compared to the guest room I was quartered in. There was just room for a narrow bed, a chair, and a tiny dresser.

A hook on the wall was empty.

The dresser contained nothing but a few articles of clothing, and those needed mending.

His bed was a thin mattress, covered with a threadbare blanket.

He had obviously moved everything he considered useful to his workroom.

I wandered back to the research facility, half intending to

revisit the scene of the crimes, but found myself at the door of Day Seven instead.

I went in, and sat in the same chair I had used before.

The Abbot may or may not have been right about all that 'deep word and spirit' talk, but I realized that it didn't matter. I had no more ideas about the killings, could think of nothing more to do that had the slightest chance of being productive. So I might as well take her advice, and think about other things.

Like that tree by the stream.

Or what part of God's creation I could . . .

I found myself thinking about ducks and rabbits instead.

About how which you saw depended on how you focused.

No—*where* you focused.

When praying I had always found God by focusing up, and a little to the left. What if I only needed to . . .?

And I already knew, because it had been there all along.

Somewhere near the middle of my back.

No. It was closer than that. Move the focus forward a bit, and . . .

Chapter 25

"We meet God reliably in only two places: externally through his creation (which includes other people), and internally as the ground of our being. Everything else is hearsay."

Sam Dean, *The Secret Diaries*

"Come."

I opened the door and stepped into the hermitage.

Pastor Dean looked up, saw the expression on my face, and grinned.

"You found it?"

I nodded.

He waved me to my chair.

"Tell me."

"I haven't thought through the details, or implications, yet, but it was like the duck/rabbit drawing."

"How?"

"So I think that it's like . . . the drawing is just lines on the paper. If I categorize those lines as a duck, I see a duck. If I categorize those lines as a rabbit—"

"You see a rabbit."

"Yes, but the Abbot showed me that my categories actually changed the way I looked, where I focused."

"Okay."

"I'm not doing a very good job of explaining this."

"You're doing fine. Go on."

"So, if it were a real duck, I wouldn't be able to see it as a rabbit. There would be way too many things about it—things I could see—that would keep me from mis-categorizing it."

"But God . . ."

"Yes. Exactly. You don't *see* God. Not in that sense. You sense him, and I haven't figured this part out exactly, but it's like you said, about me creating my own God-category, I guess, when I prayed. And I could experience God by looking up, and to the left. And for some reason, that stopped working for me. I could no longer connect that way."

"So you thought God had abandoned you."

"Yes. But it's like the tree by the stream, isn't it?"

"Is it?"

"A drought dries up the stream, but only the obvious stream —the one on the surface. The tree stays green because it's roots are tapping into the stream underground."

"And you've found your roots?"

"At first I thought the new focus was in the middle of my back. But then I realized it was actually *in* me. I can't know what it's like to be a duck or a rabbit or a cat or cow or angel. I can only know them through my categories, through the world *I* create. But I *do* know what it's like to be *me*. I know that directly—the way it is in God's creation. The closest connection I can have with God is my own *being*. And when I focus there, he's back."

He sipped his tea.

"I have two things to say about that. The first is that we—that *you*—are not done."

"What more is there to do? I'm no longer abandoned—no longer cut off from God. That's what this was all about."

"But you were never cut off from God. Remember the tree by the stream."

"I sure felt like I was."

"But why? To put it another way, who caused the drought?"

"Are you saying *I* did?"

"Look at it this way. Everything you experience—this teacup, the table, a picture of a duck or rabbit—it's all your creation, existing in your head, built out of categories that you have created. That doesn't mean it isn't real. Try spilling hot tea on yourself, and you'll see that it's all too real. You're constantly adjusting the world you create, based on your experience, to fit the real world as closely as you can. But you only experience it in a form that *you've* created."

"Right. I get that."

"And that was true of the God you created. The one that existed for you 'in front and a little above' you. That location wasn't part of the real God, but it was part of the God you created."

"Okay. And so?"

"And the real God never went away."

"But the one I created did. So *I* was the one who made God go away?"

"That much is obvious. My question to you is 'Why?' What was more important to you than your connection to God?"

"I have no idea."

"And that is why we will continue to meet. You *need* to know."

"Well, now that I know I don't know—if that makes sense—I also *want* to know. In fact, I *have* to know."

"Good. I think we should meet again very soon, now that you've had this breakthrough."

"I could come back this afternoon."

"Perfect. But let me inject a note of caution. I wouldn't talk about this experience, or at least your explanation of it, too much. There are people who would consider it close to heresy. And believe me, you don't want to deal with that. The ideas you form around it don't matter so much, anyway. It's the experience that matters."

"The experience is all I need."

But that gave me thought.

"Do you know—I should tell you—I was originally sent here on a mission to sniff out heretics. Not you—I was instructed specifically to ignore you. But apparently Presbyter Brine thought there was a dangerous group of heretics at the Abbey, and I was supposed to uncover them."

"I know. And, by the way, the Abbot knew, *and* Brother Macon. You didn't hide it very well, and it was no secret that Brine was behind your visit."

"So do you know what this heresy is? Is this—what I've experienced, all that I've been saying—is this the heresy that Brine suspects?"

"I doubt it, seriously. Brine is extremely clever in his way, but he's a purely political animal. The experience you've been going through and the ideas you've just been spouting are beyond his imaginings."

"So this has nothing to do with that?"

"There may a connection, but Brine is almost certainly after something much more literal, and he wouldn't have sent you if he didn't already know exactly what it was."

"Do *you* know what it is?"

"I'll give you a moment to think about that question."

It only took me half a moment. In all fairness, it wasn't a question I could expect him to answer.

"Forget I asked."

I HADN'T THOUGHT about my original mission much since Macon had died. But now it occurred to me that there might be a connection of some kind between my mission and the killings.

That possibility made things awkward.

I was fairly sure who the heretics were, and I was also sure that Brine already knew who they were.

And I was sure that I didn't want to expose them.

But what if I *had* to?

What if the only way to find the killer was to first uncover the heresy—and the heretics?

It didn't bear thinking about.

And yet I couldn't help it.

Brine had considered the heresy dangerous. I had trouble believing that any of my suspected heretics posed any serious danger.

And yet there were two bodies in the morgue.

That line of reasoning didn't get me anywhere. One of those bodies was Macon's, and he was at the top of my list of potential heretics. So if the heretics were the dangerous ones, why was he a victim?

Could Lilith be a heretic?

On one hand the answer was yes, easily. Lilith would never have been constricted by a love of orthodoxy. But on the other hand I couldn't imagine her caring enough about that sort of thing. She wasn't a particularly intellectual sort. I doubted she'd ever given doctrine a second thought in her life, even as a Joshuan.

So Macon's chains were probably not about heresy. Whatever the owners of those chains shared—if it was more than being friends of Macon—it wasn't just a club of heretics.

Still, I couldn't shake the feeling that my search for heresy and the killings were somehow connected.

I hiked up the trail past the bench that Lilith had used for meditation and around the bend to the cemetery.

It occupied the entire top of the hill. There was a large abstract sculpture at the center, hand-chiseled out of stone. I stared at it awhile, trying to make sense of it, but I couldn't be sure what it represented. Maybe a man, sitting under a tree? The 'branches,' if that was what they were, had spheres in them —fruit? And there was one sphere next to what would have been the man's foot. Perhaps it was an allusion to Adam and the tree in Eden. Or perhaps it's only purpose was to be beautiful. It was certainly that.

It stood on a broad flat platform, also of stone.

The graves weren't visible, because of the snow. I uncovered one, near the sculpture, pushing the snow off with my shoe. It lay flat, even with the ground, with the name of its monk hand chiseled into the surface.

I realized that the only bit of monkstone on that hill was the Bible I had brought with me.

The view was breathtaking. I could see for miles in every direction, including the entire layout of the Abbey. The path I had arrived by, after being dropped off by Brine's angel, the road winding down to the village below and working its way upward in the opposite direction to the estate houses on the next hill.

There was something serene there, and true. Something that reminded me of the sign stuck beside the path at the entrance.

———

I WAS ALMOST BACK to the common room when Brother Earnest found me. He rushed up, out of breath.

"There you are! I've been looking all over. The Abbot needs to see you right away."

"Tell her I'll be there in five minutes."

"No. *Right* away. Now."

I decided not to argue.

When I got to her office she was just finishing a conversation with one of the healers. She waved me in as he was leaving.

"Sit down, Pastor. Apparently we were wrong."

"What's going on?"

"There's been another death. One of the monks found a body at the edge of the Abbey property, not far from the road to the holder estate. It was buried in the snow. The killer had pulled her clothes off before hiding the body."

"Why?"

"Searching for something, possibly? Her underwear was still in place, so . . . The clothes were found not far away, also buried."

"When?"

"Just an hour ago. I sent Earnest looking for you right away, but he took his time."

"Not his fault. I had hiked up to the cemetery. So this body . . . ?"

"Not one of ours. Apparently it's a holder. I've sent word to the local estate, to ask if they have any missing guests. We know the family, and it's not one of them."

"So will the local police take over?"

"That's complicated. The body was found on Abbey land, so jurisdiction is fuzzy. At least until we know who did it—and know for sure who the victim is. But that's not the biggest problem, from your point of view."

"No?"

"She was stabbed in the back, with a throwing knife."

I looked at the locked door in her bookcase.

"Did you . . . ?"

"I've been afraid to. But of course we have to."

She went to the door, waved at the lock plate, and pulled it open.

The case was there, still rolled up, apparently untouched.

She pulled it out, untied the cord, and rolled it open.

There were still only two knives missing.

Chapter 26

"Could you turn the body over, please? So I can see the wound?"

The healer looked at me as though I were dim-witted.

"It's a knife wound, sir."

The Abbot was not as patient as I was.

"You heard him, William. Turn it over. Now."

He shrugged, rolled his eyes, and pulled the blanket off the body.

A holder can look more naked than anyone. The lack of a logo somehow makes them seem vulnerable and unprotected. It's ironic, since that very fact is a symbol of their power.

She was about my age or a little younger. She had probably been quite beautiful in life. She was a bit heavier than Lilith. Her hair was blond. Her eyes were blue.

I wanted to make her alive again.

The healer got the body turned, and stepped back without any more argument. My respect for the Abbot went up a notch.

The wound was horizontal, unlike the wounds on the other two.

The Abbot met the healer's eyes.

"What can you tell us about this?"

He shrugged.

"It went in between the ribs. Probably punctured a lung. She wouldn't have lived long."

"Thank you, William. That's very helpful."

She turned to me.

"The angle's wrong. I wouldn't have been able to throw that way with any reliability. And if *I* couldn't . . . "

"Maybe it isn't a question of how it was thrown," I said. "Maybe she was lying down when they threw."

"Maybe."

I addressed the healer.

"You can turn her back, now."

"Wait!"

The Abbot pointed to a spot on the back of her head.

"William. Could this have knocked her out."

William examined the injury.

"It could have. No guarantee."

She nodded to him, and he restored the body to its dignity.

"That," she said to me, "could explain the knife wound.

The killer didn't throw the knife. They knocked her down, then stabbed her."

"Why kill her in a completely different way?"

"Different circumstances? Maybe the killer was too close to her to throw accurately."

"Or maybe it was a different killer."

I decided to take advantage of the healer's cooperative mood while it lasted.

"What have we missed, William?"

He rubbed his chin sagely.

"Nothing—about this one."

"And the others?"

"Well, if the other knives were thrown, then Brother Macon's killer knew what they were doing. It would take skill and knowledge to kill quickly with a knife to the abdomen."

"And Sister Edith?"

"That could have been luck, if you see what I mean. It severed an artery, but if you were the killer would you aim at a shoulder on purpose?"

We moved to the counter, and the victim's tray. There was very little on it. Her shoes, a pair of miracle gloves, a gold armband.

The Abbot picked that up.

"Apparently our killer wasn't interested in theft."

We didn't need to unroll her clothing to see that it was expensive, and that it had been torn in multiple places.

I unrolled it anyway.

"Do you see what I don't see?"

"There's no blood. So the killer ripped her clothes off of her *before* stabbing her in the back."

"Curiouser and curiouser."

The Abbot picked up the three knives, and laid them out

beside each other on the counter. She stared at them for a moment, and then gave me a slow smile.

"These are all completely identical."

"So?"

"There are many different kinds of throwing knives. Even among the regulation ones for competition. Slight differences in the shape, in the distribution of weight, even in color."

"But these are the same."

"Whichever one is *not* mine is exactly the kind I use."

"And that's unlikely."

"Very. You realize what you have here?"

"Tell me."

"A fleecer's favorite thing. And it's the first one to appear in this entire mess."

I looked at the knives, and shook my head.

"Sorry. I don't . . ."

"*Count* them."

"Three, but . . . Oh."

"Yes. This is your first absolutely solid and complete *anomaly*. You now have something concrete that completely contradicts the world we've been creating."

"But what does it tell us?"

"It tells us that we are face to face with mystery. It tells us that we are making one or more false assumptions—that the world we are creating is significantly different from God's world—from reality. And *knowing* that is solid gold."

When Bee's body vanished I was furious. I was out for Tho's blood. But Dennis talked me down and helped me to see that I had to concentrate on Lucky's predicament first, that that was what Bee would have wanted.

He was right, of course. So I had contained my grief and focused on saving Lucky's life. In the process, Tho got what he deserved anyway.

Then I'd been distracted again, by another mystery I had to solve, and solving that led to practical problems that had to be worked out, about Boyd's mother and about Lucky's secrets.

When all of that was done, I realized what my father had been trying to tell me before he died.

And through all of it I'd had to bury thoughts of Bee in order to deal, mostly with other people's problems.

But in the end I came back to Bee.

And to what Dennis had said about the Humans 'retrieving their dead.'

I remembered the body that had started it all. The very first Human I had ever seen. And I remembered that body was still in the morgue at the police station.

No one had retrieved it.

And I realized what that meant.

Maybe the Humans didn't retrieve their dead. Maybe they only rescued their living.

Maybe Bee was still alive.

The Abbot and I walked back from the morgue together. It was noticeably warmer. Some of the snow was turning to slush.

I didn't share the Abbot's enthusiasm for anomalies.

Three knives instead of two just made the whole puzzle seem more confusing to me.

"Look," I said, "the killer had to have obtained the extra one somewhere."

"Somewhere else."

"Yes. But why? If you were going to steal two, why not steal three?"

"That's a good point. Maybe the killer already had one, but needed two more."

"But they were identical."

"And that is very unlikely."

"So the killer had to go to the trouble of finding a knife—"

"—that was exactly the kind that was in the shed."

"But if you were going to go to that much trouble—"

"—and planning—"

"—*and* planning, why steal the other two?"

"Why not just get three in the first place?"

"And why would you need the third one to match anyway?"

"So that no one could tell them apart?"

"Because," I said, "if I were to *know* which ones were stolen and which one wasn't . . . would it help me catch the killer?"

"I don't see how."

"Or maybe it would point me toward the motive?"

"I still didn't see how."

I heard the tinkling of the Abbot's chimes up ahead. We were almost to her door.

"Wait a minute. What if they're identical because they're *all* from the shed?"

"But there are only two missing."

"Right. And seven in the case. But how closely did you look at those seven?"

"Not very. I was counting them, not inspecting—Oh."

"What if the killer brought a knife of their own, maybe something like the others, but when they stole the other two something happened? Maybe they knocked some down, or—I don't know. Or maybe they did it on purpose. But somehow they left theirs, and took three of yours?"

"And, if that is what happened, then their knife is sitting in my cupboard, and may help us figure out who the killer is."

She went straight to the cupboard and got the knife case out. She unrolled it on the table, and we pulled all seven out of their pockets.

After a few minutes of examining them in detail, she shrugged.

"Nope. They're all mine, as far as I can see."

I WAS DISCOVERING something that the fleecers probably knew. It's almost, if not completely, impossible to investigate anything without a theory.

You may have an anomaly, or even an abundance of anomalies—the fleecer's 'favorite thing'—but if you don't have *some* sort of theory as to how to make sense of it, you are left without any way to form a plan of action.

I had no theory, and therefore no plan. Just a puzzle which got more complicated at every turn.

After lunch I wandered up to my room with very little purpose. I sat on the edge of my bed, my mind running in the same old circles, my eyes on the handle of my walking stick.

It had belonged to my father, and I carried it half in memory of him, and half because Bee had liked it.

The handle was a large knob of dark green stone, carved to resemble an elaborate spherical knot. My father saw it as a sort of symbol of all of life's problems—knots to be untangled. And he'd always said that the first step in untangling was understanding.

I certainly didn't understand my current knot.

After a time I grew restless and decided that, lacking any

plan, I could at least use the time for my next visit with Pastor Dean.

I left my room, and headed back toward the trail to the hermitage.

But on the way I passed Lilith's room.

On an impulse I stopped, and opened her door.

A quick survey told me that she had, indeed, been planning to take my advice and leave the Abbey. The drawers and surfaces were empty. Presumably it was all packed in her closed suitcase, which was on her bed, ready to go.

If she only hadn't made that visit to Macon's workroom before leaving.

I opened the suitcase, and probed the contents. They were not much different than I had seen before. The only thing remotely of interest was the strange golden bug which Macon had given her.

I picked it up and examined it.

It was just an ornament, as far as I could tell. It might have had symbolic value—might have meant something to the two of them. But if it did they were taking that meaning to their graves.

Something about it did bother me, though. I remembered seeing it—or a version of it—the first time I had met Macon. My memory, as brief as it was, of that bug emerging from the waters of the firmament, was different somehow—not quite the same shape or pattern.

But I couldn't say how. And, anyway, I remembered Macon granting me that self-deprecating grin and saying, "Can't always get it right on the first try, I'm afraid."

So this was just a later version.

I was now officially grasping at straws.

I closed the suitcase and continued my journey to the hermitage.

Chapter 27

"During the 'tribulation' years at the end of the Second Enlightenment, humanity came very near to exterminating itself in multiple ways. It is the ultimate irony that those who acted to avert disaster did so to preserve the property of the very class which had created the dangers in the first place."

Lois Bradford, *An Introduction to the Second Enlightenment*

PASTOR DEAN WAS FEEDING his birds again as I approached the hermitage.

I stood a respectful distance away, not wanting to scare them off, until he noticed me. He opened his door, and waved at me to follow, so I did.

The birds kept right on eating as I passed them.

He settled into his chair, and I sat in mine.

"Well," he said, "what has become clear to you since our last meeting?"

I realized that he probably didn't know about the holder's body. So I filled him in on that before moving to my personal issue. It took some time, and the new developments seemed to worry him, though he didn't explain why.

Finally I got around to the real reason for my visit.

"To answer your original question, nothing has become clear to me since our last meeting. Certainly nothing about these killings, but also nothing about our topic here."

"You haven't lost ground? You still understand that the God you were praying to before your 'abandonment' was actually your own creation?"

"So I wasn't praying, really, at all."

"Nonsense. The 'Pastor Dean' you're talking to right now is also your own creation, and in exactly the same sense. Do you believe you aren't really talking to *me* at all?"

"But I have a lot better, and clearer, evidence of who *you* are."

"That's true enough. It's much easier to form your internal 'Pastor Dean' to fit the real Pastor Dean than it is with God. But the real question is your intent."

"My intent?"

"Every person who prays begins with the exact same problem. We pray to a God of our own creation, just as you converse with a Pastor Dean of your own creation, or drink from a teacup of your own creation."

"But with God . . ."

"With God, it's easier to fool yourself. So, in the end, the difference from one prayer to the next is how much the person praying really wants to connect to the real God. Some people— all of us, at one time or another—only want a God that confirms what we want to believe. About ourselves, about the world, about others."

"Yes. I've wanted that. But usually praying put a stop to it."

"It doesn't for everyone. You value truth more than most, so the God you created—"

"—was impossible to lie to."

"And that helped you not to lie to yourself."

"Until it went away."

"Until you *sent* it away."

He picked up the teapot and took it to his altar, but continued talking.

"I've counseled a lot of people, Adam. A lot of pastors. And many of them have experienced what you went through, one way or another. Their own version of the absence of God.

"I don't pretend to have the final word on this, but I will tell you what I've come to believe. All of those people had dispensed with the God of their own creation—not consciously, any more than you did—but they each had their own reasons.

"Some of them had already discovered what you have discovered—the closer connection within themselves—and so they simply didn't need their own creation anymore. Those came to see me just to be reassured that they weren't crazy.

"Some had come to need that deeper connection, and so had found their own creation wanting, inadequate to their need. Some deep instinct within them had realized that they couldn't go deeper without letting go of the security their own creation provided.

"And some came into conflict with their own creation. Something about the God they had fashioned had become impossible to live with.

"That last group comes in many different forms. Sometimes it's a curse. By moving away from their own creation they are also moving away from the deeper connection. Sometimes it's a blessing. They find the deeper connection sooner than they might have otherwise.

"If I had to guess, I would say that you are in the third group—and one of those for whom it was a blessing. I believe you have really found that deeper connection. But even if you have, there's no guarantee you'll keep it. We are, after all, creators by nature, and the temptation is always there to create another God of our own. The first step in escaping that temptation is to understand why you abandoned the God you created."

He returned with a filled pot and a cup for me. The steam rose between us as he poured.

"I could be wrong about you, but I don't think I am. So humor me. Assume that you sent your own creation away because you had a conflict with it. What do you think that conflict was?"

"I haven't a clue."

He took a sip.

"Well, think about it. Think about the nature of the God you created, and why that God might have become intolerable to you."

WE PARTOOK of our last tasteless meal that evening, each of us by then looking forward with heightened expectation to the feast promised by the morning and Resurrection Day. The Abbot asked if I would lead the community in the closing prayer at the morning ceremony. I said I would.

On my way back to my room I paused at Lilith's door, but could not think of any good reason to go in.

Instead, I continued to my own room and my own bed.

My dreams were confused and anxious. A tangle—of

knives I couldn't seem to count right, of bodies laid out in the morgue, of Earnest's grin, of stone sculptures I didn't understand, of a golden bug, of Lucky leaving, of Lilith and Bee and Macon's magic and my missing aunt. And somewhere, hovering in the background, the menacing eye of Presbyter Brine, and the uncomfortable sense that I was sitting on a soaking wet bench.

I awoke with the memory of Macon, drunk on Stoneseve, snoring on the floor where I left him.

It was already getting light outside. I leapt out of bed, dressed quickly, and hurried down to the service.

It hadn't begun yet, so I was saved that embarrassment.

The Abbot motioned for me to stand next to her, since I would be participating in the ceremony, and I took my place by her side. She was holding a large bunch of flowers. We waited while a few more stragglers, later even than me, found their places in the circle.

When everyone was present, the Abbot smiled and began by reciting the passage from scripture.

"And it was at dawn on the morning of the third day that his closest followers saw that the guards were there no longer, and they came to the pile, to remove the stones and to bury him. And they labored long at the pile, for his enemies had been many, and those who had remained true were few."

She handed the flowers to Brother Earnest, then stepped into the center of the circle, lifted a stone, and brought it back to place on the ground. When she straightened Brother Earnest gave her one of the flowers, then turned and handed the bouquet to the monk beside him. Then he stepped into the circle and followed her example.

And so around the circle, all in silence. Until we all held flowers.

When it came full circle to me, I realized that there were

two flowers, and two stones, left. It was obvious that the Abbot hadn't anticipated that—any more than I had.

I made a quick decision.

I handed the flowers to the Abbot, stepped into the circle, and lifted both of the remaining stones.

The ground underneath was now bare, the stones having completely obliterated the drawing in the soil.

Something about that tugged at my memory, reminding me of Macon, drunk Macon. What had he said?

I lugged the stones back to the circle and placed them on the pile.

The Abbot held out both blossoms to me, keeping her own in her other hand, and gave me a brief smile acknowledging my decision, then finished her recitation.

"And lo, when they had finished removing the stones his body was not there. For he had conquered death."

She turned to me, and I continued.

"And his followers knelt there and prayed, as he had taught them, saying . . ."

And everyone joined in the recitation of Joshua's prayer.

"Our Father, who lives in the sky . . ."

And that was the moment at which I began to understand.

THE REST of the ceremony was a blur for me. My mind was racing, re-evaluating everything I had learned from Macon, from the Abbot, even from Pastor Dean.

Even, for that matter, from Brine himself, sitting on that soggy bench.

I struggled to remember the details of those conversations. It had been explicit in my first counseling exchange with Macon.

It had been the point of much of his eccentric teaching. The magic tricks, the talk of creation, even his last drunken words to me had all had a single point.

I was oblivious to the decorations that had been added to the tree in the common room, to the bows of greenery adorning the mantle.

I could hardly contain myself during breakfast—a real Resurrection feast that any other time I would have remembered for the rest of my life.

I hardly noticed it.

I couldn't wait to get alone, to put it all together in detail, to get it straight in my thoughts.

And even at that stage I could sense that it somehow held the key to my other puzzles.

Finally the feast ended.

Finally I could escape to my room.

I started by opening my Bible to the first creation narrative —the one Macon had spent so much time on.

And yes. It was there. Plain as day. I was mystified that I had ever missed it, that anyone could.

Next I turned to the second narrative and the idea that had bothered me at the center of the stone circle. I knew what Macon had said now, and I knew what it meant. And once again I was astonished that I hadn't seen it before.

And that reminded me of the other thing he had said that night. I looked up the genealogy of Joshua. I read it through to the end and found what I had only vaguely remembered—but which had been Macon's point.

Clear as a bell.

But the clearest hint of all had been handed to me on a silver platter by Brine, before any of this had begun.

That bothered me.

And I began to understand why three people were dead.

Chapter 28

"My research moves forward, and I am also learning the theory behind the monkstone algorithm. Fascinating. I do have trouble understanding why it is so important to use the word 'spirit' instead of 'energy,' or to call every process, procedure, form, or structure a 'word.' But the equations still make sense, so I suppose the terms aren't that important."

Michael Kinde, ancestor of Adam Kinde

I HAD NEVER INSPECTED the site where the third body was found, so I headed out to the road, and when I got there, I followed it uphill, keeping my eyes on the Abbey land.

The day was much warmer than the previous day, and the walk was actually pleasant. Birds chirped in the trees along the side of the road. The sun shone down and glistened on the snow—which had even disappeared in random places.

I found the spot I was looking for easily. The healers' ambulance had used the road to get there, and the body had been carried to the ambulance by hand, so there was a path of trampled snow and dead vegetation leading me from the edge of the road to the spot where the body had been.

I spent some time searching the area in the interest of thoroughness, but it seemed there was nothing more to be found, and I had already seen what I needed to see. So I retraced my steps to the road, then back to the path leading to the Abbey.

It was the same path I had walked up when I first arrived. I remembered how cold it had been, reading the little sign off to the side, watching Lilith's back as she walked ahead of me.

And I remembered other things I had seen that day—and the thing I hadn't.

THE MORGUE WAS LOCKED up tight, of course. It was Resurrection Day, and even the healer's clinic had only minimal staff on duty.

I hiked back to the common room and found William sitting rather sullenly in a corner. He didn't seem to be enjoying himself at all, so my request was easier to make.

It wasn't well-received, however.

No matter how little he was enjoying the party, he found letting me into the morgue to be even less pleasant. And he made that plain.

Luckily the Abbot spotted us arguing, and crossed the room to weigh in on my side of the question. So in the end William grudgingly accompanied me back to the morgue, and unlocked the door.

I went in, and he followed—standing just inside with his arms crossed, indicating both that I needed watching and that he wasn't going to volunteer any help.

My first interest in coming there was the arm-band that the holder had been wearing, so I crossed the room directly toward the counter that had held the trays of possessions. Consequently, I was halfway across the room before I noticed the empty tables.

Lilith and the holder were both missing.

I changed my direction, forgetting the arm-band, and I came to a stop next to the table that had held the holder.

I put my hands on the table to steady myself, and stared.

Stared straight into the reflection of monkstone light on bare metal.

I HAD FOUND Dennis in his tiny office at the end of the corridor. He was in charge already, as senior detective, but he hadn't yet been promoted to chief.

He wasn't impressed with my reasoning. I could tell that.

I explained that he had been wrong about the Humans retrieving their dead. That, if that were true, they would have retrieved the body downstairs in the police morgue. That the fact that they hadn't could only mean one thing. They had taken Bee, not because she was dead, but because she was still alive.

He pretended to listen, but I knew he was humoring me, that he thought it was all just wishful thinking.

I was adamant. Bee was still alive, and we had to find her. And the only source of information that could help us was the other Human—the corpse in the cellar. Something about that body would tell us where to look, what to do next, how to find Bee.

Finally he agreed, probably just to get rid of me, but I didn't care why.

He led me down the steps, took me to the morgue.

And there, where I had expected to find the clue that would lead me to my love, was an empty table.

I put my hands on it to steady myself and stared.

Stared into the reflection of monkstone light on bare metal.

Dennis tried his best to find out what had happened to the body, but no one knew. As far as anyone in the station knew no outsider had visited the morgue.

It should have still been there.

The healer in charge had assumed that the body had been released without his knowledge. He had only stopped short of leaving, outraged at that violation of protocol, because Chief Tho had just been executed and there was no current chief to blame.

I was disappointed, of course, that we had lost our main source of information about Humans. But I was determined to find Bee by other means if that was what I had to do. Dennis didn't believe she was still alive, but I could get him to search for my aunt. She would know.

———

"Pastor?"

I lifted my eyes from the table, and tried to make sense of my surroundings.

"Pastor? Are you all right?"

It was William. I was in the morgue. I had come to see if the armband . . . But the bodies were gone. All but Macon's.

"Pastor?"

"Yes. Sorry. I'm fine. It's just that . . . they're not here. The bodies. They're gone."

"I could have told you that back at the common room. Saved us both a trip—if you'd let me get a word in."

"Where are they?"

"The bodies, sir?"

"Yes the bodies! Don't play games with me today, William."

He uncrossed his arms.

"The holder's relatives came to collect her yesterday afternoon. We weren't told to refuse them."

"No. You weren't. The relatives were from the estate up the road?"

"Yes sir. We know them well, you see. They're very supportive of the Abbey, and they use our healers. It didn't occur to me to question the request."

"Of course not. And Sister Edith?"

"The Joshuans sent a chariot to collect her."

"When?"

"A little earlier than the holders."

I glanced at the empty trays, each with a throwing knife next to it.

"And their belongings went with them?"

"Yes."

I sighed.

"Well, William, let's get you back to that party."

I STILL HAD access to the research facility and Macon's workshop, so I didn't need to bother anyone else for that.

The building was completely empty because of Resurrection Day celebrations, as far as I could tell. I let myself into

Macon's workroom once again, and once again I surveyed the chaos.

I knew who, and I had a good idea about why. The how was trickier.

The air in the room was still a bit fetid, the smell of blood after that first metallic scent has faded. I decided to mask it by making a pot of coffee.

Macon's altar still held its blessing, not having been used much, and he had the necessary supplies in store, so I had the room smelling better in short order.

I poured myself a cup, and sat down to consider.

It was tempting to try to recreate the killing in my head one more time, but that had got me nowhere in the past so I resisted the temptation. I concentrated on trying to recreate that moment when I'd had that thought—the thought that I hadn't been able to pin down.

It had to have been after he was killed. I was here, alone in his workroom, and . . .

I looked around. His drawing board? The coffee-pot? Neither of those. The coin trick? That duality link?

I surveyed the shelves, and spotted the Shadow deck.

That rang a bell.

Instead of reaching for it, I lifted a box from the worktable, and pulled out the sketch of a card.

That had been it. It was when I realized how he did the trick with the cards. You thought it was something he just did, off the cuff. But it actually required a great deal of preparation, and he had been prepared all the time.

I remembered him standing there the first time I entered, the look on his face as he reversed the process of the firmament and the golden bug was reabsorbed.

And then I checked one last thing.

I passed Lilith's door on the way to my own, and remembered knocking on it with the good news about Pastor Dean's angel.

I remembered looking up to see her at my door, and the rush of feelings I had then.

When I got to my room, I stood in the doorway, remembering her kiss. Remembering how I pulled away, and why. And how I might not have, if I had allowed myself to know what I now knew.

Then I put my mind to the task before me.

At first glance it wasn't there, but I had to be absolutely certain before taking things any further.

So I turned the room upside down, searching everywhere it could conceivably be.

I checked all of the surfaces, the drawers, my suitcase. I checked the bathroom and the bed table. I looked under the bed, and under the dresser.

I looked everywhere.

And found nothing.

Absolutely nothing.

It wasn't proof, but it was pretty close.

And part of me didn't want to know. But I couldn't make that mistake again.

It was time to take the leap.

Time to put out a fleece.

Chapter 29

"Ralph has been charged with heresy and dismissed. I don't understand exactly what the charge was based on, and I don't think he does, either. Perhaps I should be paying better attention to the theology taught at my church if I want to survive professionally."

Michael Kinde, ancestor of Adam Kinde

THE WIND-CHIMES TINKLED outside the Abbot's office.

I had looked for her in the common room, where everyone was celebrating, but she wasn't there, so I assumed her office was the next best place.

I opened her door, and stepped inside.

She was at her table, bent over her Bible, stylus in hand.

I stopped across from her, hands on the back of a chair, and waited.

Finally she looked up.

"Pastor."

"Happy Resurrection Day."

"And to you. Thank you for your quick thinking at the service this morning. It wouldn't have been good for Sister Edith's stone to be left sitting there."

"I thought it was best."

"And I'm sure it wasn't the easiest moment for you."

"No."

She shot me a quizzical look.

"Is something wrong?"

"I need your help."

"What can I do?"

"I need you to come with me to Brother Macon's workroom."

"I'm at your service."

She pushed her chair back, stood, and walked past me to the door.

We passed the circle of stones where the services had been held, the pond which was showing signs of thawing, the chapel —which I realized I hadn't set foot in during my whole visit— and we came to the door of the research facility.

Inside we walked down the corridor, past the murals, then along the covered walkway to the door marked 'Master Wright.'

She opened that door, and we went in.

She glanced around the room.

"I'll be glad when this is over, and we can clean this place up a bit. Did you make the coffee?"

"I did. Would you like a cup?"

"No, thanks. But I'm glad you made it. It helps. With the smells."

She walked around the firmament, to the center of the room.

"What do you need me for, Pastor?"

"You told me, when I first came, that you could operate the firmament."

"That's right. I'm the only one here now who can. I suppose I'll have to add that to my duties until we find a new master wright."

"I need someone to help me re-enact Macon's death. And since you are the only one who knows how the firmament works . . ."

She stepped behind the tray, where Macon had stood on the day I met him.

"You think he was making something when it happened, then?"

"I do."

"But there wasn't anything there when he was found. And the firmament wasn't even on. So you think the killer took whatever it was with them?"

"I don't."

"I'm sorry. I'm not following this."

"I'll try to explain as we go. Can you start it running?"

"It won't make anything very elaborate. Not without a disk."

"Just use the one in the tray."

"It's a blank."

"If I'm right it just hasn't been labeled yet."

She gestured in the air, and the firmament emitted a low hum.

"Just make whatever the disk makes, then?"

"Yes. But be ready to stop it the second I tell you."

She nodded, and gestured again.

The hum changed its note to a higher pitch.

"So why are we doing this?"

"Because I think I was wrong from the beginning. I only

had three suspects to start with: you, Lilith, and Earnest. And I didn't want any one of you to be guilty. Particularly not you or Lilith. I think that clouded my thinking. It all seemed to boil down to who had access, and to who could throw a knife."

"Doesn't it still?"

Something was slowly rising out of the liquid in the firmament. It was a kind of ridge at the center, along a line from the Abbot to the door. It was curved slightly higher at its center.

"Not if I'm right."

"Really?"

The object rising out of the liquid was showing more shape now. It looked like one edge of a very large thin doughnut.

"Think about the last victim. The holder. That knife almost certainly wasn't thrown."

The doughnut was now about halfway out of the liquid. It was only a couple of inches thick. And it was clear that the bottom half didn't continue to curve. So the thing was shaped more like an upside down U.

I had a better view of this than the Abbot, because I stood at the side of the firmament. She could only see something that curved away from her, toward the door.

"Right. We knew that one wasn't thrown. But what about the ones in this room?"

The leg of the U farthest from the Abbot, the one closest to the door, appeared to be crumbling. Bits were dropping of its surface from a spot about ten inches above the liquid down to where it was emerging.

"I don't think those were thrown either. And more to the point . . ."

The surface fell away, like a snake shedding its skin, and what remained was the shape of a throwing knife.

I looked up at the Abbot.

"Stop! Now!"

She made the same gesture that Macon had made that first morning as we entered the room.

But the object kept growing. It actually grew faster.

The tip of the blade broke free of the liquid, and the U snapped straight up.

I shouted "Look out!"

But I was too late.

The blade broke free and shot straight at the Abbot's head.

She went over backwards, and as I rounded the firmament I found her lying where the others had, on her back, in a growing pool of blood.

***

Pastor Dean opened the door of the hermitage with a look of surprise.

"Adam. Isn't it a bit close to lunchtime for a visit?"

"I need your help."

"Of course. Come in."

"I need you to come with me."

He searched my face for a moment, then nodded. He crossed to his table, picked up his Bible, and followed me out the door.

"I can only come so far, you know."

I handed him one of the two baskets I was carrying.

"Can you go as far as the bench on the trail without alerting your guardian?"

"I can do that."

"Good."

We hiked up to the main path, then turned toward the cemetery. When we got to the bench, we stopped and sat down.

"So what can I do for you?"

I put my Bible on the bench beside me, then took his Bible from his hands and put it on top of mine.

"Trust me."

I stood.

He gave me a questioning glance, but followed suit.

I hiked on toward the cemetery.

He followed.

We hadn't gone more than ten feet when the angel appeared.

"FEAR NOT! The hermit must honor his solitude."

I thrust a palm toward the angel's face. I doubt that Pastor Dean had any idea how brave that was.

"I am an ecclesiastical judge, presiding over the investigation of three deaths on these premises. I have need of this man in my inquiry. I will return him to his solitude as soon as I am through with him."

"The hermit must honor—"

"Do. You. Doubt. My authority?"

The angel glared at me for a moment, then faded away.

We continued hiking.

We arrived at the top of the hill to find the Abbot had already cleared the stone at the base of the statue. She had spread out a large picnic blanket there, and was seated on it.

The bandage around her head hid the wound the knife had made.

We set the baskets down and joined her. I pulled a corkscrew and a bottle of wine from one of the baskets.

Pastor Dean stared at the bandage.

"What happened to you?"

"I had a little accident while helping Pastor Kinde with his investigation."

"Yes," I said. "And I'm very sorry. I should have anticipated that."

"So what are we doing here?"

I pulled the cork from the bottle.

"Abbot, do you have your Bible with you?"

"No. You asked me to leave it behind."

"Thank you. We're going to have a little picnic. And while we do that, we're going to conduct the first of two inquiries into the deaths of Brother Macon, Sister Edith, and a stranger to our community. This will be the real inquiry. Later, the official inquiry will be held in public."

I poured the wine into three glasses.

"But let's begin with a toast. To the memory of Brother Macon, of Sister Edith . . . Lilith, and the holder who died on Abbey land."

We clinked glasses and sipped the wine.

A cloud passed between us and the sun for a moment then moved on.

"Now," said the Abbot, "who wants an egg salad sandwich?"

She passed them around.

I laid out food from the other basket. Cheese, crackers, potato salad, baked beans. And I passed out some plates and utensils.

We concentrated on our food for a time, but finally Pastor Dean broke the silence.

"So when does this inquiry begin?"

I took a sip of wine and swallowed the last of my sandwich.

Chapter 30

"I SHOULD TELL YOU," I said, "if you don't know already, that I am as certain as I can be that no one—not even an angel—will be listening in on us."

Pastor Dean raised an eyebrow.

"How do you know that?"

"Most people carry their Bibles with them at all times, and in most places there are Joshua statues erected at regular intervals, so we tend to assume that angels can go anywhere. But it turns out that angels can only appear—or eavesdrop—in areas close to certain objects made of monkstone.

"And I'm pretty sure there's no monkstone on this hill."

The Abbot concurred.

"We only use hand-carved natural stone here. It's to honor our dead. Even the sculpture of Saint Isaac was done completely by hand, from natural stone."

I continued.

"So we can dispense with the usual caution, and speak openly.

"I'm required to say—even though there will be no official record of this meeting—that this is not a civil hearing, that we are here as a community of clergy, and that our purpose is not punishment, but to decide on the best course forward for all."

I addressed the Abbot.

"The night before he died, Brother Macon asked me if I was an agent of the 'big O.' Do you know what he meant?"

The Abbot started to shake her head, but Pastor Dean put a hand on her shoulder.

"Yes," he said. "We both do. And so do you."

"I have a general idea, but I need you to fill in the details."

"How much do you know already?"

"I know that you said long ago to forget I'd ever heard the name Osseus. I know that Brine is heavily connected to Osseus. I know that Osseus is involved in some very corrupt and illegal business. And I know that he—or *it*, or *they*—had something to do with the death of a person I loved."

He leaned back against the statue of Saint Isaac and stared into the clouds overhead.

"How many people have you told that to?"

"None. And what you say here will go no farther."

He exchanged glances with the Abbot again, then met my eyes.

"What do you want to know?"

"What Osseus is, for a start."

"We don't know. Sometimes it seems to be a person. Sometimes it seems to be a group. It operates in secret, behind the scenes."

"What does it do?"

"Things it shouldn't. Things no one should do. Much of that is political, one way or another, and has to do with wielding or gaining power. Osseus was almost certainly behind my conviction of heresy—for a heresy I never held, by the way. My real sin seems to have been simply knowing that Osseus existed."

"So you aren't really a heretic?"

The trace of a smile formed on his lips.

"I never held the heresy I was *charged* with. Osseus has left his, or its, or their stench on too many ruined lives—promising careers destroyed, promising projects undermined, reputations ruined, families destroyed. Even violence of various kinds.

"So I have no trouble believing that Osseus was involved in the death of your loved one, or in the deaths of Sister Edith and Brother Macon, if that's what you're asking. We know way too little. But we're determined to learn more, and to do something if we can."

"We?"

His eyes flicked toward the Abbot, and she nodded her consent.

"At this point, 'we' means the Abbot and me, for all practical purposes. It used to include Macon and our newest member, Sister Edith. A little group Macon dubbed 'the Linklings,' after the chains he made us and some obscure reference to the Dark Age which only he understood. There are others, but Sister Edith was our only connection to them."

"What about Dr. Thomas?"

"My brother-in-law and my sister haven't been in touch since I became a hermit. It isn't really safe for them to know me. But you're right. He was involved the first time you heard the name. I'm sure he's still out there, fighting the good fight."

"So Sister Edith was one of you?"

"Yes. When Macon connected with her at that conference, he discovered that she knew about Osseus, and had other contacts who also knew. He had taken a couple of his chains with him, in case he found others, and he gave her one."

"Do you know why she was visiting the Abbey?"

"She was involved in an attempt to get a lot more information. Osseus uses encrypted communications, and Macon agreed to create a device that would decrypt the messages. She was coming here to collect it."

"Something like this?"

He took the golden bug from my hand and examined it.

"Probably. Macon called it the 'goldbug'. Another of those playful allusions—like 'the Linklings'—which only he understood. So this fits that description. I have no idea how it works, though."

"And neither of you told me any of this because . . ."

"In our situation you learn to be very cautious. I hadn't seen you in years. While I seriously doubted that you would ever have anything to do with Osseus, I wasn't the only one involved. You *were* sent by Brine. And of course we knew, almost from the beginning, that you were looking for heretics, which had a very Osseus smell to it."

He tossed the bug into the air, and caught it again.

"Later, when people were being killed, we were pretty sure

that Osseus *did* have an agent at the Abbey, and you were the only outsider present."

"We couldn't," the Abbot added, "completely ignore the possibility that you were that agent, no matter how little we wanted to believe it."

"Well," I said, "you were right to be cautious. There were *two* of Osseus' agents here the whole time, and I was one of them."

Chapter 31

"Kinde was nearly incapable of rationalization. He saw contradictions clearly, and refused to ignore them, no matter how uncomfortable they were."

Silas Redford, *The Real Adam Kinde: An Experiment in Biography*

"I was sent here," I said, "as the entire world seems to have known, on a secret mission to unearth a heresy and some heretics. There was no reason in the world why Presbyter Brine should think I was a good choice for that kind of mission. The fact that I couldn't keep my mission secret for even twenty-four hours just underlines that. I had no experience in espionage, or even minor deceit. And I was no expert on heresy.

"When Brother Macon was killed, and I was promoted to

ecclesiastical judge, I was even more surprised. I have neither the training nor the experience to be an ecclesiastical judge.

"So I was in over my head from the beginning. Even though I had three suspects who *could* have done it, I couldn't see any reason why any of them would have *wanted* to do it. Sister Edith only knew Macon from a single conference and from a rather bland correspondence. Neither Brother Earnest nor the Abbot seemed to have any quarrel with him at all, in spite of Lilith's claims.

"As it turned out, I was quite right about that. None of the three had any serious reason themselves to desire Macon dead.

"Meanwhile I was still half-heartedly trying to figure out what that heresy was—a heresy that Brine had told me was extremely dangerous. And there was the complication of the knives, which went from one to two to three, and seemed to completely defy logic.

"I was at a loss, and it stayed that way until Resurrection Morning, and the end of the ceremony. The Abbot had asked me to lead Joshua's prayer, and suddenly everything that Macon had taught me clicked into focus. I knew exactly what the heresy was."

Pastor Dean and the Abbot exchanged a glance.

I continued.

"And as soon as I knew that, I also knew Pastor Dean was right when he suggested that Brine *already* knew. Because Brine had given me a very strong hint before he sent me, though I hadn't realized it at the time. He had also provided me with a list of suspects—focusing my attention on Macon and the Abbot.

"I hadn't been sent here to discover the heresy or the heretics. I had been sent to be the ecclesiastical judge investigating killings—killings that Brine knew were going to happen before they did.

"So in one way I already knew who the killer was. It was Brine, or people closely associated with him. They had arranged the killings, and put me in place as their unwitting agent to blame the person they wanted blamed.

"And I had no doubt who that person was. She was a famous knife thrower, and she had access to the room where Macon was killed. I hadn't already accused her for a variety of reasons, but there had never been any question that she was the chief suspect.

"So I came to the conclusion that I had been put in place to accuse the Abbot, who was actually innocent. But I still needed to figure out who did throw the knife, and how they managed to get into the room."

I looked at the Abbot.

"That was where your teaching came in handy. I realized that the extra knife wasn't the only anomaly I was dealing with. There were other anomalies as well—large ones and small ones, positive and negative."

"Negative anomalies?"

"Yes. The extra knife was what you might call a positive anomaly. Something that shouldn't exist in the world I had created in my head but which showed up anyway. But I was also helped by the opposite of that. Things which *should* have been, but weren't."

"An interesting distinction. I like it."

"I had been ignoring most of those because they didn't fit my own created world and also, I suspect, because I didn't want to think about their implications. But once I realized that Brine was manipulating me, I let go of the world I'd previously created and began to notice things I hadn't noticed before.

"I remembered arriving just behind Lilith and watching her walk up the path in front of me. Except there was no sign of the chariot which had brought her. A negative anomaly.

"I remembered seeing Macon watching her as she entered the Abbey. Another negative anomaly."

"Negative?"

"They were friends. Yet he just watched. He didn't attempt to wave at her, or shout hello. Odd, don't you think?

"And Lilith avoided meeting her friend Macon. She claimed to take her meals in her room because she was on a spiritual retreat, yet she showed no other signs of seeking solitude—she convinced you to give a throwing demonstration, and spent a great deal of time talking to me.

"Macon made no attempt to see her either. They used me as a go-between, even for the exchange of gifts."

I reached over and took the Goldbug back from Pastor Dean.

"Macon's gift to Lilith was no secret. She had no trouble letting me see it. But her gift to Macon was nowhere to be found. I spent quite a bit of time in that workroom, and I should have noticed if something new was added to the clutter, but I couldn't find a thing that stuck out.

"When I added all of those to the anomaly of the knives it was as confusing and frustrating as trying to identify one of your red spades, Abbot. None of it made any sense at all. I couldn't see any pattern.

"Then I remembered this."

I held up the disk Macon had given me as a spiritual exercise.

"Macon used this in one of his magic tricks, then gave it to me, to use for a spiritual exercise. He instructed me to keep it with me at all times, so that I would constantly be reminded of that trick, and of the spiritual lesson it contained. I showed it to Lilith, and told her that it was from Macon.

"But there was a second disk, one I found on the floor after Macon was killed. I picked it up, but didn't think it relevant.

When I got back to my room and I realized I was still carrying it, I put it on my dresser and forgot about it.

"I searched my room for that second disk this morning, and couldn't find it. And that was when the duck finished turning into a rabbit for me. A new story took shape in my mind, and everything finally made sense."

Chapter 32

"By a stroke of luck the department chair is in my denomination. He wants me to join the new monastic order. The long-term plan is for all scientists to be monks and theologians. And celibate, though here's a special exception for married men who join early. If I wait it might mean finding a new career."

Michael Kinde, ancestor of Adam Kinde

"I was an unwitting agent for Brine, and probably for Osseus, but there was another agent at the Abbey from the beginning, a conscious agent who orchestrated all three deaths. She was very intentional, very skilled, and very clever. And she completely fooled all of us.

"The reason I didn't see Lilith's chariot drop her off that first morning was that she hadn't just arrived. She had arrived much earlier. But instead of entering the Abbey she had waited on the road for the real Sister Edith, who happened also to be a relative of the local holder. She knocked her out, removed her clothes—which she needed to be whole and bloodless—and stabbed her with the knife she had brought with her. It was intentionally identical to the Abbot's knives, so that it would look like the Abbot was the killer.

"Lilith then put on Sister Edith's clothes, which were only slightly too big for her. She could wear everything but the arm-band, which wouldn't stay up on her arm. She ripped her own clothes—probably so that no one would notice they were too small for Edith—and buried them nearby. She took Sister Edith's suitcase, and by the time I was arriving she was on her way up the path to the Abbey.

"Macon didn't wave to her because he could see her face, and he knew immediately that she was an impostor. If he'd had any sense he would have warned the two of you, but he was a man who loved intrigue and game-playing."

"That's true," the Abbot said, "It would be just like him. And you are the perfect example of that. Even though he knew you were on a heresy hunt, he couldn't resist giving you one hint after another."

"Exactly. In Lilith's case he created a fake Goldbug to give her. I don't know whether he expected her to accept it as the real thing, or whether he wanted to see how she would react when she realized it wasn't.

"She sent him a gift in return. An unmarked disk which Osseus had prepared for her. She, and those who sent her, counted on Macon's curiosity, and he didn't disappoint them. He was probably cautious, and ready to stop the process at any moment, just as I was when the Abbot helped me with our little fleece. But he made the same mistake I did. He didn't antici-pate that the word on the disk was designed so that it couldn't be stopped. That the attempt to stop it would actually speed it up.

"The disk created a device to throw a knife directly at the person standing in position to control the firmament. And it was successful. It not only wouldn't stop on command, it also was designed to be reabsorbed by the firmament immediately and to turn the firmament off once that had happened—leaving no trace."

"Except," the Abbot said, "a knife exactly like my own."

"Lilith had already arranged for you to invite me to that throwing demonstration, for two purposes. She made sure I knew how well you could throw, and she took the opportunity to steal and hide two of your knives—so that we would think the ones found with the bodies were yours.

"Everything went as planned, and it would have been successful, except that Lilith didn't check the Goldbug until after she had given me the package for Macon. When she did check, she discovered it was a fake. So she needed to find the real one, which she had been instructed to bring back with her. That was when she remembered this disk."

I held it up again.

"She guessed—I think correctly—that Macon had hidden the disk that made the real Goldbug by giving it to me. He knew me well enough by then to know that I would follow his instructions and keep it with me—and if I hadn't told Lilith about it, that would have been a brilliant hiding place.

"So she searched my room. And there, on the dresser, was the disk I had picked up next to Macon's body. The murder weapon.

"She took that disk to the workroom, convinced Earnest to let her in, and as soon as he was gone she tried to recreate the Goldbug. I don't know where she learned to use a firmament, but she clearly did."

"It's not tricky," said the Abbot. "Not if you're just using a prepared disk."

"Well, in any case, I don't think she had ever seen the killing device work before, because she didn't anticipate her danger until it was too late. The knife, which was designed to hit Macon's abdomen, hit her in the shoulder because she was that much shorter. Later, when we put out our fleece, it just grazed the top of the Abbot's head."

"I'd never really considered my diminutive height to be a blessing before that."

"So," I continued, "Lilith was dead, which made it harder for us to suspect her. But now there were three knives, which made it harder to believe the story we'd been telling ourselves."

"An anomaly we couldn't miss."

"Exactly. So, unless either of you questions these findings, I am ready to make my ruling and close this inquiry."

"But why," said Pastor Dean, "didn't the Joshuans notice that Lilith wasn't Sister Edith when they picked up the body?"

"My guess is that her relatives at the estate had already told her order that they had the body. So the 'Joshuans' who picked up Lilith's body were really from Osseus."

I gave them another moment. But neither said anything, so I continued.

"I find that the killer of Sister Edith and Brother Macon and Lilith was an agent of Osseus, that the final responsibility for those deaths are shared by that agent, by Presbyter Brine, and by Osseus. As it is not in the interests of this community to make those findings generally known, I also find that this verdict will remain a secret between the participants of this inquiry."

Chapter 33

"Funny how decisions are made. The monastery will be allowed a fireplace. It's only in the common room, so it won't be like winter evenings at home in the past. But I think the family will outvote me, even if I resist. So I guess we'll be moving."

Michael Kinde, ancestor of Adam Kinde

We packed up the picnic and headed back to the Abbey, stopping at the bench to retrieve the Bibles we had left there.

The angel appeared without any proclamations, watching us with an accusing glare.

It took us a few seconds to rearrange our loads, and add the Bibles to them. Somehow our packing up had been much less gainly than the packing in had been.

The Abbot, who had packed more carefully, stood by and watched our struggles.

Then she pointed at the slope behind the bench.

"Take a look at that!"

There, about three feet back from the trail, only half covered by the disappearing snow, were two throwing knives.

I stepped around the bench and managed to retrieve them without slipping and falling.

The Abbot was astonished.

"She thought we would never find them there?"

"More likely, she planned on retrieving them and taking them with her."

I held them up to the angel's eyes.

"Have you seen these before?"

"I have."

"When?"

"When the sister put them there."

"Why didn't you tell me that when I questioned you about her?"

The angel just looked confused.

Later that afternoon I went with the Abbot for my final visit to Brother Macon's workroom.

I handed her the coin that Macon had given me, and she placed it on the tray in front of the firmament. Then she made the appropriate gestures, and the process began.

It was slower than the knife throwing device, probably because the word for it was more intricate and complex, but in the end Brother Macon's creation slowly emerged from the waters below.

It looked a great deal like the bug he had gifted to Lilith, but it was less attractive, and seemed more pragmatic in its design. Calling it a "Goldbug" would have seemed whimsical, or at least metaphorical, if I hadn't seen its counterpart. The legs had odd ends on them that looked functional in some way, though I couldn't have guessed what that function was.

The Abbot seemed pleased.

We made a second one, as a backup, for me to take with me.

I used Macon's tools to mark that disk with a large *G* for Goldbug, and I marked the other disk, which had still been on the tray, with a *K* for knife. I didn't want those two to get mixed up again.

I left the *G* disk with the Abbot, and kept the *K* disk as a souvenir.

I kept Macon's chain and the fake Goldbug as well.

WE SCHEDULED the official inquiry for the following morning. It was the first time I had seen the inside of the Abbey chapel.

It was lovely.

The pews were natural wood and looked handmade. The altar was simple, plain, and dignified. There was a large clear window behind the altar, framing an old tree just outside. The walls to the left and right were lined with stained glass windows, alternating images from the life of Joshua with images of various saints.

I noticed one of Saint Isaac there, much like the statue in the cemetery, sitting beside a tree. There was a moon above him in the daytime sky. An apple was in the air next to it, falling from the tree.

It was a serene and quiet place. A place for contemplation.

The inquiry progressed without incident. I questioned various parties about the events of the previous week, asked for any additional input from the community, and handed down my official verdict.

Everyone seemed relieved to have it all resolved.

My work done, I hiked up the hill to the hermitage, and my final visit to Pastor Dean.

He asked me if I had any more thoughts about my remaining question.

"You mean why I abandoned the God I created?"

"What made you need to abandon that God, yes."

"I know exactly what it was."

He watched me silently until I continued.

"The God I created was primarily a God of truth. It was impossible for me to lie to myself when I was in prayer—when I was in the presence of that God. It had served me well— keeping me from believing things just because I wanted to, or because I felt I *should* believe them. And that was really good for me."

"Until?"

"Until I needed—needed more than anything—to do just that. Fool myself. Let myself go on believing something that I shouldn't have. Hold on to a fantasy, not because it was true, but because I so much wanted it to be true. That was when I couldn't connect with my God anymore, because connecting would mean admitting something I couldn't admit."

"But you have, now."

"Yes."

"And it's painful?"

"Oh, yes."

"I'm sorry."

"Thanks."

"Do you think that old God will return now?"

"I don't think so. I have a deeper connection. I don't need that one anymore."

He smiled.

"You're right. You don't. Can I change the subject?"

"Sure."

He put one hand on his Bible.

"You should keep Macon's belt, as a souvenir. I think you qualify as one of his friends now."

I didn't see the need to tell him I already had it.

"Thank you. I think so too."

"The symbolism of the duality links isn't the only significant thing about those chains he made us."

"No?"

"Think about it."

THE FUNERAL for Brother Macon was held that same afternoon, also in the chapel.

I didn't speak. There were many there who had known him both longer and better.

They told stories of his conjuring tricks, of his strange sense of humor, of his eccentricities, and mostly of his generosity and friendship and love.

They made affectionate references to his size, especially when seen walking next to the Abbot.

He was a man who didn't compromise much, but never seemed contrary, a man of integrity and playfulness and depth.

There were multiple comments about the clutter in his workroom, as well.

Chapter 34

"Some have argued that his findings at the Abbey were clearly mistaken or that he intentionally misrepresented events. Such views are completely out of character for a man who put such a high value on the truth."

Silas Redford, *The Real Adam Kinde: An Experiment in Biography*

BRINE'S CHARIOT picked me up the next morning after breakfast.

I walked down the same path I had come in by, to meet it at the road.

On the way I stopped to read the little sign I had seen that first day:

Saint Isaac's Abbey
No Hunting
Except for Truth

I stepped into the chariot, and was surprised to see Brine sitting there, waiting for me. He didn't say anything, but gestured toward a seat.

I put my suitcase down, leaned my walking stick against a cushion, and sat.

Brine nodded to his angel, and the chariot rose above the Abbey, as smoothly and silently as it had arrived.

We rose over the Angeles Forest, and picked up speed on our way back to the Valley.

After a while, Brine spoke.

"I must . . . ahhh . . . must apologize. For dropping you . . . dropping you so precipitously into such . . . such . . . ahhh . . . heavy responsibilities. Unfortunately, it couldn't be helped."

"I understand. I just hope I managed them well."

"How did the inquest go?"

I was quite sure that he already knew exactly how the formal inquest had gone, but I played my part.

"It was rather complicated from my point of view, though I did my best to put everything in the simplest terms possible for the sake of those attending."

"And what . . . what did you find complicated?"

"The first death—Brother Macon's death—seems to have been caused by a device he was creating. The Abbot is a champion knife thrower, and the two of them were friends. One explanation could be that Brother Macon was inventing a device that would throw knives—possibly to challenge the Abbot to a contest. But the device malfunctioned and killed him while it was still in the firmament. It had been reabsorbed before we found the body, and the knife it threw was just like the Abbot's knives, so at first I suspected her.

"Then the second death occurred. Sister Edith—a Joshuan on retreat—managed to get into Brother Macon's workroom and activate the device a second time. It killed her as well. And by that time I had discovered that there were two knives missing from the Abbot's collection."

"So you . . . ahhh . . . you continued to suspect the Abbot."

"I did."

"And this Sister Edith, I understand you knew her from . . . from another time?"

"She used to be my girlfriend. In my last year of seminary. It's been a strange week. A lot of coincidences."

"There were other coincidences?"

"The hermit at the Abbey turned out to be Pastor Dean. You'll remember him. He taught at the seminary."

"Yes. He was also your . . . ahhh . . . childhood pastor. A heretic. I tried to protect you from that."

"And I would have taken your advice. But unfortunately I had asked for spiritual counseling. That got me into the Abbot's good graces, and she even assigned me to Brother Macon, which gave me regular close contact to him. Which was all very useful. But she eventually assigned me to the hermit as well. It couldn't be helped."

"I see. An interesting tactic, though. But there was . . . ahhh . . . a third death, was there not?"

"Yes. Another one—or actually two—of those coincidences. A member of the local holder family was killed at the edge of the property that same week."

"You said *two* coincidences?"

"The knife which was used was also identical to the Abbot's knives. That seriously confused matters for some time."

"Could the Abbot have actually been behind that death?"

"I had to consider that, of course. But you see, we found the two missing knives, so it was very unlikely. Another coincidence, by the way. I have no idea who took them, or why, but it's obviously unlikely that it had any direct connection to Brother Macon's ill-conceived device."

"I see . . . see what you . . . take your meaning, that is, about . . . ahhh . . . about coincidences. So there was no . . . no guilty party?"

"Except for whoever killed the holder, but there's no reason to believe that had any connection to the Abbey. It happened right next to the road."

"So the inquiry is closed, as far as the church is concerned. What about the other . . . ahhh . . . the *original* mission I sent you on?"

"That was much simpler. I know exactly what the heresy was, and who held it."

Chapter 35

"Wealth is power, knowledge is power, force is power, and freedom is power. Power leads to conflict, and conflict to chaos. The remedy is to isolate. Let the well-bred mind our wealth; the clergy, our knowledge; the state, our use of force; and let none enjoy freedom."

Oss Taylor, founder of Mens Dei. Final address to the First Committee

"You have discovered the . . . ahhh . . . the heresy?"

We were past the Angeles Forest now, headed into the Valley. The brown grid of squatter land stretched out below us.

"Yes," I said. "It's quite remarkable really, and quite as dangerous as you predicted."

Brine sat up a little straighter at that.

"Dangerous?"

"In two ways, really. First, because it is very convincing, and very obvious—or should be—to anyone who takes the scriptures seriously. It begins in the creation narratives. The first narrative repeats the idea of all life forms—from plants to fish to birds to animals—reproducing 'after their kind.' That is, when they have children, those children are like the parents. You know, the way you say that someone is 'the image of his father'?

"Then, on the sixth day, it says that God made humans in his own image. I'm really quite surprised that I hadn't ever heard anyone comment on the natural implication of that—that humans are children of God, and that we are, therefore, divine.

"And in the second creation narrative it says that when God created the first human from the soil, he breathed the breath of life into him. In other words, the human spirit and the divine spirit are one and the same.

"It becomes even more convincing in the teachings of Joshua. Remember telling me about that heresy you confronted when you were younger? The idea that Joshua may not have known he was divine? And your response was that he must have known, because he called God his father?"

"I do ... ahhh ... "

"Well, that argument, the very one you made, would apply equally to all of us. Because Joshua taught his followers—taught *all* of us—to call God our father. So it would follow that Joshua taught that we were *all* children of God, that we were, in fact, Gods, just as the children of an owl are owls, and the children of dogs are dogs.

"And that isn't all. Because the genealogy of Joshua traces his heritage back to Adam, who it then says was the son of God."

"You sound as though . . . as though you have . . . ahhh . . . convinced yourself."

"Do you remember the question you asked me to contemplate before all this started?"

"Question?"

"About why your reasons for thinking that Joshua knew he was God were not the *right* reasons?"

"Ahhh. I see. You have an answer?"

"A heresy is not a heresy because of scripture. It can't be, because there can be disagreements about how to interpret scripture. A heresy is a heresy because it isn't orthodox."

"And orthodoxy is . . ."

"Orthodoxy is whatever the church *says* it is."

"I may have underestimated you. Who held this heresy?"

"Brother Macon, who is dead."

"What about the Abbot?"

"We had far-reaching conversations, and she never uttered a heretical word, whereas Brother Macon was constantly hinting his beliefs to me. I can't read the Abbot's mind. But if she *is* a heretic, she has absolutely no interest in making converts."

"So she is . . . ahhh . . . no danger. And the second reason that this particular heresy is dangerous?"

"It's dangerous because of what it implies. If each person is divine in their own right, then there is no need for the authority of the church. The entire ecclesiastical structure would lose its purpose and its power."

Brine was silent for a very long time then. When he finally spoke again, he was slow and thoughtful.

"Yes. Underestimated. I think we should be giving more thought to your advancement. For a start, let me . . . ahhh . . . let me say that I will probably forget . . . yes, forget . . . to reverse your access levels, and I think we will make your promotion to ecclesiastical judge a permanent, or at least an ongoing . . . ahhh . . . ongoing status for now."

He nodded to himself, and then to me.

"What was the nature of your . . . your spiritual problem?"

He probably already knew that, as well.

"I thought I had lost contact with God."

"And did you regain this contact?"

"Yes and no. The God I had known was my own creation. I didn't create a replacement, if that's what you mean."

He nodded sagely.

"If I may . . . ahhh . . . may offer a bit of my own counseling. One's own spiritual experience is not . . . not all that *reliable*, if you see what I mean. Obedience is the thing. Discernment is tricky at best. But obedience . . . Obedience is . . . the only truly *safe* route."

Chapter 36

"The only good dog is an obedient dog."

Oss Taylor, founder of Mens Dei. Final address to the First
Committee

I HAD Brine drop me off in front of the police station in the village. The desk sergeant waved me through to the beige hallway, which had lost most of its fresh-paint odor. I found Dennis in his office, sitting behind his desk. I could have sworn he hadn't moved since I last visited.

I put my suitcase down just inside his door, and surveyed the room.

"Something's different."

He laughed.

"It's the chairs."

Sure enough. There were two very comfortable-looking

chairs on my side of the desk. The former chief had forced everyone to stand in front of him while he sat.

"So it is."

"Have a seat. It makes things more pleasant for everyone, don't you think?"

I sank into the nearest one, and emitted a little sigh.

"It's good to be back."

Dennis lifted his chin at my suitcase by the door.

"You haven't been to the parsonage?"

"I'm afraid I'm putting it off. Do you know if Lucky . . .?"

"No. I didn't keep track. He may have gone. He may not have. He may even have gone and returned. Did you have a successful trip?"

"It's hard to know. I think I could say that my mission was successfully completed in more ways than one, but I lost two friends."

"Alienated, or . . ."

"Dead."

"I'm sorry."

I shrugged.

"What's new around here?"

"Almost nothing. I bought those chairs. If you mean about your aunt . . ."

"I didn't."

"Well, there's nothing there, either. We'll keep trying. You hungry?"

We ended up walking over to the Humble Monk for lunch. It was good to be back among the clatter of dishes and conversations and the valiant efforts of the proprietor's Bible to make the national quartet's rendition of "Trust and Obey" heard above them.

We talked a little church business, he told stories about his kids, I gave him a description of the Abbey and a very incomplete account of the events there. We laughed a lot during that long conversation, and I realized that was something I hadn't done for months.

After lunch I walked back with him to get my suitcase. I had half-planned to go see Boyd at the Franklyn estate next, but I realized that my chariot was at the parsonage. And then I realized I was just putting off the inevitable.

THE GRASS on the parsonage lawn had been freshly mowed. I could smell it on the air as I approached. So I knew that Lucky was home.

I went in the front door, and straight up the stairs to my bedroom, where I unpacked my suitcase.

I took my Bible and my souvenirs from the week to my office, and put them on my desk. Then I flopped into my desk chair, and stared out the window at the treetops beyond.

After a while I shifted my gaze to the great chain Brine had gifted me with, hanging on the wall opposite. It was beautifully made. Different from the chains that Macon had made. More ornate, but no more artful.

I wondered what Pastor Dean had meant about a second significance in Macon's chains.

But mostly I just sat there for half an hour or more, thinking almost nothing, half recovering from my recent adventures and half dreading what I still had to do.

Eventually I dragged myself from the chair and crossed to the wardrobe at the end of the room. I opened the doors, pushed the clothes to one side, pressed the correct spot on the back panel, and rotated the rod the clothes hung on.

The panel snapped back and I slid it out of the way,

revealing a series of secret shelves which held my meager and illegal book collection.

I went back to my desk and selected the Goldbug and the disk marked *K*. I put those on one of the shelves, next to my second—also illegal—Bible, then I slid the panel closed, pulled the clothes back into place, and closed the wardrobe doors.

There was a knock on the door.

I dropped back into my chair.

"Come on in, Lucky."

Lucky pushed the door open and came to stand in front of my desk. He managed to combine the look of an errant child, a defiant servant, and a judging parent all at once.

"I went on that trip I told you about, lad. Went while you were gone."

I didn't reply. He continued.

"I did it without your permission, and I'm not sorry. It was something I had to do. I understand if you're not happy about that, but I did tell you. I've mowed the lawn and cleaned the place. There's enough food in the kitchen to last you a week or so. You should be able to find a replacement by then."

I looked at Macon's belt then, and at the sculpture on the wall.

I shook my head, and sat up straight.

"I'm sorry, Lucky. It should never have been an issue. But I was confused about something—about a great many things, really. If you needed to do it, you needed to do it. And you didn't need my permission."

His face relaxed, and faint wrinkles appeared at the corners of his eyes.

"No hard feelings, lad?"

"None. Was your trip a success?"

"It was. I'll tell you about it sometime. When the time is right."

"When you're ready."

He stopped at the door on his way out, and turned back to face me.

"Welcome home."

"You, too."

I listened to his footsteps on the stairs, then turned my attention back to the sculpture on the wall. Every link a person —or at least the office a person held—all joined from top to bottom, from most important, most powerful, to least. Each level owing obedience to the one above.

I picked Macon's belt up and examined it. There was no hook or latch or buckle. Just a continuous loop of chain. All of his chains had been like that. No way to tell one end from the other, or top from bottom. Each link in its own position, and all connected—all equally important to the integrity of the whole. And each one the image of the Holy Duality.

I walked around the desk, lifted Brine's gift from the nail which held it in place, and hung Macon's belt in its place.

Then I wrapped Brine's chains around the sculpture at the top, and put it all in an empty drawer.

I FELT like I had crossed some ill-defined bridge, into an unknown land wreathed in mist. I had no categories for the inhabitants I would meet there or the paths I would travel.

I sank back into my chair, and gazed at the branches outside my window.

The Abbot would probably have said I was having an encounter with mystery, and that may well have been true.

There was so much I didn't understand.

And so much grieving I had left to do.

I didn't know how to connect the Lilith I had once loved—

or at least had *thought* I loved—with the Lilith who could kill a stranger in cold blood.

But I grieved her, nonetheless.

And I grieved the loss of Brother Macon: Brother Macon of the eccentricities and conjuring, of heresy and humor, of clutter and of Stoneseve drink.

I hadn't known him long enough to claim him as a friend.

And yet I did claim him.

Perhaps it isn't the length of a friendship that matters. Perhaps it isn't even how personal the sharing has been. Perhaps it's only the mark that the friendship leaves on you.

I was not the same person. And that was due to friends. To Pastor Dean, of course, and to the Abbot as well, but also to Macon, to that giant of a man. That trickster and guru, that teacher and friend.

And deep down, beneath my grief for him, was the loss of Bee. The loss I couldn't accept, and so couldn't grieve, for so long. She, too, had left an indelible mark in a very short time.

Eventually it began to get dark outside. I could hear Lucky's distant whistling in the kitchen as he prepared dinner, and could detect the faint scent of cooking drifting up the stairs.

And then I thought of the one person I could never properly grieve, because I had never known her. The real Sister Edith, who could never be more than just a body in the morgue to me.

She had a family who did grieve her, of course. Holders— her relatives next to the Abbey and her closer family elsewhere.

I pictured her visiting her parents on her childhood estate, perhaps stopping off there just over a week ago on her way to visit her other relatives, the ones who lived near the Abbey.

But there was something wrong with that picture.

An anomaly.

Her father and mother wouldn't have worn a logo; they were senior holders. But she would never be an heir, not after entering the church—we were not allowed to hold property, none of us. So she could never be a senior holder, and she would always have to wear a logo.

Except that she hadn't. Not on her forehead or even on her hand.

I remembered Lilith explaining about the headband, that the Joshuans used it to cover their logos. But Lilith wasn't a Joshuan; she had almost certainly been improvising a lie.

And then I knew.

The headbands weren't worn to cover a logo. They were worn to cover something else entirely—to cover the fact that Joshuans *don't* wear logos.

I knew, then, where to look for my aunt.

The End

If you want to read more about Adam Kinde, just leave me your email address at krwatts.com/th-ge and I'll send you advance notice of the next book and a free copy of the series prequel, *Human Unforgiven.*

Also by K. R. Watts

The Guardian Dolphin

Parables from the Grave

Human Unforgiven

The Human

About the Author

K. R. Watts is the author of two series, *Philosophical Fantasies* and the *Adam Kinde Alternate Future Mysteries*. He graduated from California State University at Northridge and received an MA in theology and a Ph.D. in philosophy from Fuller Theological Seminary in Pasadena. He and his wife, Virginia, have two children and three grandchildren.

krwatts.com

www.ingramcontent.com/pod-product-compliance
Lightning Source LLC
Chambersburg PA
CBHW050830190726
48286CB00007B/2026